Pirate Island

Find your pirate bravery!

Katie L. Carroll

Katie L. Carroll

Published by Shimmer Publications, LLC

Cover illustration by Sue Tait Procaro

ISBN: 9780998925400

Visit the author's website at www.katielcarroll.com

To David
My first writing buddy
Hot chocolate is still on me

Chapter 1

As I sit here alone on the beach (well, as alone as I can be since the infamous Captain William Kidd began possessing me), Pirate Island looms dark against a bright blue sky. It's the place where my dream of finding Kidd's lost treasure will be fulfilled, and his dreams of I'm-not-sure-what may also come true, hopefully not at my expense. My mortal body has already had one close call on account of Kidd.

I'm waiting for my sister and her stupid boyfriend to show up. So long as they come ready to dig, I don't care who they are. The sun has yet to dip below the horizon. The steady rhythm of lapping waves is usually a comfort, but nothing can soothe me right now. My skin prickles with anticipation, or maybe the sensation is Kidd's. It's gotten hard to tell who's the source of each feeling.

I'm responsible for being numb-thumb deep into the search for treasure. My best friend Andy may have started it, but it was me and a long-dead pirate who got me (us) numb-thumb deep into this mess.

Andy used to be the one who would force me into

things. One night we were having one of our marathon video-game sleepovers. I kept saying we should go to bed, but Andy insisted on one more game. Pepped up on energy drinks, one more game turned into two, which turned into three, which turned into twenty. Before I knew it, the sun was rising and we were still playing.

My thumb had gone completely numb, and then it cramped up so badly I couldn't use a pen for days. I almost failed a math test because of it.

Numb-thumb deep is a real commitment. And it was usually me who would get bogged down in the quagmire, while somehow Andy would sail clear away from the swamp, like he could control the winds.

But it's all William's fault this time. What I mean to say is I got myself into this mess, but I'm not sure who or what I am anymore. I used to be a kid named Billy: good student, obedient son, pain-in-the-neck little brother, loyal best friend. Now I go by William, same first name as Kidd, famed pirate who died over 300 years ago, though everyone thinks I'm into using the more grown-up version of my name. William answers to no one but himself...and the pirate who is possessing him.

Am I channeling Kidd's spirit to be brave? Is he using my body to do his bidding? Maybe both, maybe neither. We haven't really worked out the terms. It's a relationship that's as fluid as the waters of Long Island Sound, which are currently parting to reveal a sandy path.

Technically it's a tombolo, but everyone around here calls it a sandbar. Most of the time it's covered in water, but twice a day at low tide, the waters recede enough to create a thin strip of sand from the shore all the way to Pirate Island.

That's the path I'll take to riches, fame, immortality. Which of these are my desires and which are Kidd's? That's another thing I'm not sure about. Our wants are woven together tighter than the fibers of a rope. Doesn't matter anyway. As long as we find the riches. Tonight.

Though it has not yet risen, the last full moon of the summer is tonight, and I'm on the final leg of this mystery. But as I wait for my fellow treasure hunters, I'm thinking of beginnings. All endings start somewhere. And William's began with Billy, whose adventures always used to start with Andy.

Chapter 2

Weeks prior, Andy strode into our summer writing class like he owned the library, even though I had it on good authority—namely Andy's—that he hated to read. It was 9:59 a.m., and he was the last to arrive…as usual.

I was in the back of the library's conference room, arms dangling to the side gorilla-style, drying out my pits over the air conditioner. Andy's eyes bugged out when he saw me, and I quickly clamped my elbows shut.

Seemed everything I did lately amounted to social suicide. He was probably worried a girl might see and my dorkiness would rub off on him.

He winked at a table full of giggling girls—sweet, beautiful-as-the-rising-sun Ella Platt among them. Andy shook out his shaggy hair and headed to the back of the room. While I got my hair buzzed every two weeks, he was letting his grow out. "That's what the girls like," he had told me.

I would've needed a second air conditioner for the back of my neck if I let my hair grow that long. But since summer had started, he cared more about impressing girls than about being comfortable. The question was did he care more about girls than about his best friend. That was what I had yet to find out.

Ella's gaze followed Andy to our usual table, then to me. I dropped my stare to my sneakers, my face burning brighter than lightning. I might as well have posted all over the Internet that I had a crush on Ella.

Maybe I should've posted about my crush status. It might have been the only way Ella Platt would have noticed scrawny me next to Andy (this was before I became half-boy, half-pirate William). Back then I thought the only way I could impress her was with my writing.

Mortified, I slipped into the seat next to Andy and noticed how he towered above me even sitting. Had he grown again? His proportions were reaching epic scale, his arms almost as thick as my legs.

I snuck a peek to find Ella was still watching Andy, as were the rest of the girls at her table. Our teacher, Mrs. Shields, clapped her hands. Ella whipped her head around, silky brown hair swinging slightly with the movement.

Andy turned a glare on me. "What if she had seen your monkey act?"

My cheeks warmed. Had she seen me? "She didn't," I whispered, not convincing myself, never mind Andy. "No big deal."

"She better not have." There was a menace to Andy's

tone that told me I'd regret embarrassing him.

I tried to listen to Mrs. Shields talk about developing interesting characters, but Andy started his usual fooling around, forming tiny spitballs under the table. I wondered —as I had all summer long—why he was even in the class. It was a voluntary class, and my seventh-grade teacher had recommended I take it because I enjoyed creative writing. I think Andy's less-than-awesome performance in English had something to do with him being here.

School was the one thing I was better at than Andy. He kicked my butt in football, his favorite sport, which I quit playing last year. He spanked me in gym soccer, even though I played on a competitive team and he didn't. Baseball at the park, pick-up street hockey, backyard badminton. Name the sport, he was better.

It wasn't just sports either. Andy always won when we played video games, card games, and most board games— except Scrabble, which he never wanted to play. And we always ended up doing what he wanted.

As if I needed help being invisible.

But he had been my best friend since...well, his family had moved to the neighborhood when we were babies.

The story goes that my mom brought over a casserole, the dish in one arm and me in the other. Andy's mom, holding him, answered the door. He reached out, grabbed my hand, and said, "Friend." It was his first word. I just about puke every time I hear that story, though we have been best friends ever since.

Being Andy's best friend used to be awesome. Who doesn't want to be best friends with the guy everyone wants to be around? Being in his very presence made you feel cool...until it—he—didn't.

I had grown tired of how he bossed me around and bested me at pretty much everything. Except school, I thought I had Andy on that one.

"Psst, Billy." Andy poked me in the arm. I ignored him.

"Ahoy, matey," he whispered like he was some kind of pirate.

I continued to ignore him until a sticky, slimy spitball smacked against the side of my neck. "Landlubber," he whispered loudly.

A second slimy glob hit my cheek. Hitting me with spitballs was a bit much, even for Andy. I figured I'd better answer before he attacked again.

"What?" I asked out of the side of my mouth.

"Avast," he said. "Meet me on the main deck after class."

"The main deck?"

"It's...part...of...a...ship," he said real slowly, like I was stupid for not understanding his gibberish. "Just meet me in the research section after class."

Andy, the kid who never studied for a test and barely

made it out of seventh grade, wanted to do research at the library?

"Why?" I asked, hoping the answer wasn't going to be building a machine that destroys stuff—mainly, my life.

"Arrgh. Pirate treasure." The quirk of his lip and the glint in his eye told me there was more to it than that.

Mrs. Shields glanced in our direction.

"Let's talk about it later," I whispered.

I wasn't sure what kind of pirate treasure Andy expected to find at the library. He was up to something. And I would probably go along for the adventure, like I always did. His crazy schemes usually turned out to be fun, when they weren't threatening to ruin my life.

Chapter 3

When Mrs. Shields called for a five-minute break, I turned to Andy expectantly. "So what's the deal with your pirate talk?" I refrained from rolling my eyes, an action sure to earn me a punch on the shoulder.

Andy cracked his knuckles and took his sweet time answering. He loved making me (everyone) wait. "I know where we can find pirate treasure."

"You think there's pirate treasure at the library?"

"Well, not really. But what we find there might lead us to pirate treasure."

I was surprised that he seemed to have a plan. I shrugged like I didn't care, but I was curious. "I don't know."

Mrs. Shields clapped her hands. "Break's over."

"Just do it, Billy," Andy said loudly.

I glanced at the table of girls and breathed a sigh of relief when none of them looked our way. Then I narrowed my eyes like I was deciding on my own terms what to do, but I was scared of getting in trouble during class. Andy had no problem making a scene to get what he wanted.

Before I could answer, a tanned, delicate hand placed a thick stack of papers in front of me. I snapped my head up to find Ella smiling at me, the fluorescent light on the ceiling shining above her head like a halo. In a soft voice, she said, "Mrs. Shields asked me to hand these back."

It was the story I had been working on all summer about two best friends who find out a ghost lives in one of their attics. Mrs. Shields had written on the top page, "Fun story! Very imaginative. Keep up the good work."

I slid the stack closer to Ella, thinking maybe she'd see Mrs. Shields's compliment, but she only handed a single sheet of paper to Andy. He quickly folded it a bunch of times and shoved it in his pocket. Still, I saw the red words scrawled across the paper. "See me after class!"

Knowing it was mean to find joy in my best friend's failure, I hoped that Ella had seen what was written on Andy's paper. I needed all the help I could get in the girl department.

When Ella went back to her seat, Andy turned to me with wide blue eyes. He steepled his hands, held his fingers to his lips, and mouthed the word "please" like he was praying.

"Fine," I whispered. "I'll meet you later."

Then I rolled my eyes at myself. I was such a pushover. But maybe he was serious this time. If we did manage to find pirate treasure, well, that would certainly get Ella's attention.

Instead of listening to the other students reading their work aloud, I zoned out. I pictured us standing on either side of a treasure chest, gold coins spilling out over the edges. A TV crew capturing the moment for the world to see. The large crowd clapping and cheering. Ella's silky hair blowing in the breeze, eyes on me.

If only that was how it played out, but now I know things never go as we imagine them.

Chapter 4

When Mrs. Shields dismissed class, Andy jumped up like he had been sitting on a barbed-wire fence. I actually know what that looks like.

I had once seen him stab his butt on a barbed-wire fence at the town dump. He'd heard that some super rich lady had accidentally thrown out a bunch of really valuable jewelry. He decided we might find it at the dump if we went after it closed. Turns out the dump was guarded by a pair of underfed Rottweilers with appetites for human flesh that rivaled the hungriest zombie. We barely escaped with our butts intact. That was the scariest thing that had ever happened to me in my whole life, and we never did find any riches.

As Andy raced over to talk to Mrs. Shields, I drummed my fingers on the table, intending to wait there and eavesdrop on him getting in trouble.

He glared at me. "Get out. I'll meet you when I'm done."

I scuffed my feet on the floor, debating whether or not

to tell Andy where he could stick his pirate treasure. Instead I quietly crept from the room and retreated to the non-fiction section. I glanced over the books while I waited. A couple about ghost sightings caught my attention. I'd check them out later, when Andy wasn't around. He sometimes made fun of me for reading so much.

Then Andy was right next to me, as if thinking about him too many times had summoned him. The short hairs on the back of my head prickled and I rubbed them until they stopped.

"What're we looking for?" I asked in a quiet voice. Something about this section of the library made me want to whisper extra quietly.

"A treasure map," Andy said.

"Where do we find that?"

He snapped his fingers a couple of times. "I've gotta check the computer listings. Chill here for a sec."

All through class I had wondered where he thought we might find treasure. Pirate Island came to mind. Everyone and their mother (literally) had searched it for infamous pirate Captain William Kidd's treasure…back 20 years ago. Once endangered birds started nesting there shortly after, no one had been allowed on the island. Beachgoers were permitted to use the tombolo out to the island, but it was illegal to set foot on it.

I couldn't imagine how we'd pull off going there, never mind digging up treasure…if there was any treasure. I mean, if no one had found it after all those years of looking, was there really any loot there to begin with? I waited to see if Andy could pull a rabbit out of his hat or if it was all smoke and mirrors like usual.

He strode back, a scrap of paper in his hands. "Billy boy, we are minutes away from finding a map to the great lost treasure of Captain Kidd."

I studied his over-confident grin and suspected my smoke-and-mirrors theory was right.

If only I had known why he wanted to find treasure on Pirate Island, I might have understood his persistence, but it would take a lot for me to discover Andy's true motives. Desperate people do desperate things for the ones they love.

All I said was, "Captain Kidd? You're kidding, right? You know it's illegal to go on Pirate Island."

"Never stopped me before."

True, the law was not something Andy let get in his way. But there was a difference between sneaking into an old dump full of garbage no one cared about and defacing the home of endangered birds. The DEP patrolled the waters around Pirate Island regularly. I was not interested in getting mixed up with a government agency.

Still, I followed Andy to an aisle in the back corner of the library, like an obedient best friend.

He produced a folder from his backpack and flipped through a book from the shelf. I tapped my foot while I waited, thinking that I should leave but staying by his side, ever the captive audience.

"I've got it!" he finally cried.

Instinctively, I hissed, "Shhh," which Andy ignored.

"Look at this." He showed me a page with a hand-drawn map of an island. He pulled a crumpled photo from the folder. "This is an aerial shot of Pirate Island. And check it out, the map in the book matches."

"Give me that." I studied the page and sighed with annoyance. All I had to do was read the caption to see that it wasn't Pirate Island. "This is a map of Madagascar, which is like a million times bigger than Pirate Island."

Step up and see the Amazing Andy. Smoke and mirrors. Smoke and mirrors. Polite applause.

"Hang on." Andy stood and pointed at the ground. "Wait here."

I am your biggest fan, I think, and I'll wait all day for the end of the act.

I stayed and browsed through the articles from his folder. They were all about Pirate Island and its history. How the Paugusset Tribe spent their summers there, back in the 1600s, and later how some lady ran a summer resort. And of course, all the legends about Captain Kidd burying his treasure and how no one had ever found anything. But lots of people claimed to have seen his ghost. And reports of people hearing strange drumming sounds from the island. And seeing eerie lights at night. Creepy, definitely. But hardly evidence that there was anything there worth digging up. More likely, it was a bunch of people's imaginations gone wild.

As I skimmed through more articles, I found a few dated from just over 20 years ago about professional treasure hunters who had wanted to dig on Pirate Island. They had scanned the whole island with special equipment and got what they called "a positive result." They were never allowed to dig because shortly after, the government closed the island to people.

I had always thought the rumors of treasure were just that: rumors. But maybe there was more to it. I began to read more carefully.

One of the professional treasure hunters was quoted as saying, "Our equipment doesn't lie. Something is there under the earth. We are being denied the opportunity to dig and discover the truth about a centuries-old mystery."

My skin prickled with building excitement. I imagined slipping a gold ring with a big, gaudy jewel on Ella's finger, her hair blowing slightly in the salty breeze (somehow it was always windy when I pictured her in my imagination), and the sun setting behind us as we clasped hands.

I was staring into space, the articles strewn all around me, when Andy arrived back in the aisle. He dumped a pile of books next to me.

I shoved the articles in his face. "Have you read these?"

He shrugged. "Sure. A little."

"Did you know that professional treasure hunters detected something buried on Pirate Island and wanted to dig to find out what it was, but weren't allowed?" I asked in one breath.

"Duh? How else did you think I knew Captain Kidd buried his treasure there?"

"How do you propose we get on the island?" I was really drilling him, seeing how seriously he was taking this.

"We're just a couple of kids. No one will notice if we do a little exploring, especially if we go at night." He held out a fist. "Numb-thumb deep?"

I knocked my fist against his. "Numb-thumb deep."

Goose bumps peppered my arms. Maybe his idea would actually pay off.

I should have known better, but I was too busy pulling a smoke-and-mirror job on myself.

Chapter 5

"Where'd you get that picture of Pirate Island?" I asked as we waited for the librarian to check out our books.

Andy shrugged. "My mom sent it to me."

Andy's parents got divorced earlier in the year, and his mom moved all the way across the country to Arizona. He stayed at my house for two weeks right after it happened. It was pretty cool to have him as a roommate, except for all of his messes. He had seen his mom only once since the divorce.

My parents get along fine, probably because they are so busy they don't have time to fight. My dad is a super important lawyer and always has meetings with clients, even on weekends. My mom goes with him a lot because she works part-time in his office. Not having my parents around is nice sometimes, but it isn't exactly great when they leave my sister in charge. Kristina can be so bossy.

The computer beeped and the librarian cleared her throat. "Andrew Walker. You owe three dollars and ten cents in overdue fees."

I was surprised Andy had borrowed books from the library, but I wasn't surprised they were overdue.

Andy looked at me with his wide blue eyes. "Can you spot me the money?"

I shoved my hands in my pockets and came up with one quarter, two pennies, and a ball of lint. I placed everything but the lint on the counter. "That's all I've got."

The librarian looked down at us and cleared her throat again. "I need three dollars and ten cents…or a library card with no overdue fees to let you take these books."

"I have a library card," I said. The librarian held out her hand. "The thing is I don't have it with me."

"What's your name?" she asked.

"Billy…William Bonny."

(Pretty soon I would be going by William all the time, but then it was only for official things like library cards and school documents.)

Her fingers clickety-clicked over the keyboard. "Here you are. William Bonny, cardholder in good standing." She scanned the books and slipped them across the counter. "They're due back in four weeks. Take care to return them in time to avoid the late fees."

As soon as we were out of the library, I held out the books for Andy to take.

"They're for you," he said.

"What do you mean, they're for me?" I asked, arms

still outstretched.

"I need you to do the research."

I stomped my foot. "Wait a sec. This was your stupid idea. And now you want me to read all these?"

It was a good thing we were outside because my voice wasn't exactly library quiet.

"I start practice tomorrow," he said. Andy is the quarterback of his super-competitive football team. He practices five days a week and has games on Sundays. My weekly soccer practices and games are easy in comparison. "Besides, you like to read. I bet you could get all these books done in like two days."

My best friend is really smart about getting what he wants. Even though I try to hide it, he knows how much I liked to read. And I *was* interested in learning more about Captain Kidd and his buried treasure.

"Fine." I tried to sound reluctant, but it came out high-pitched like a dog's yip when its tail has been stepped on.

Stack of books teetering in my arms, we walked to my house. Andy avoided looking past the backyard as I opened the side door with my key.

Before his parents got divorced, Andy lived diagonally behind me. To get to each other's houses all we had to do was squeeze through a hole in one fence and hop another. After the divorce, Andy's dad sold the house and they moved to a condo across town. Now it was a 10-minute drive or 20-minute bike ride to visit each other. Somehow living farther apart made the friendship harder.

I wanted to swim in the pool. Andy said he had to save his energy for practice, so we watched TV in my air-conditioned living room. My mom came home from the office to drive Andy home, and I went along for the ride. I was always going along for the ride.

Back home I got to work on the stack of books on my bedroom floor. Andy was almost right about me reading the books in two days; it actually took me the rest of the day and the next two days to finish them all.

Most of the books painted Captain Kidd as a typical pillaging, murdering pirate. With one biography left to read, I was starting to think the whole idea of treasure on Pirate Island was a legend not worth digging into. I pulled the last book from the stack and a puff of dust flew right into my face. I coughed and hacked, and the book dropped to the floor. I ran down to the kitchen and downed an entire can of soda in seconds. Still, I couldn't get rid of the tickle in my throat.

Back in my room, the book lay innocently on the floor, open but spine up. It was late, so I hopped over it and into bed with the intention of leaving it for the next day. That's when I began to cough again. My throat felt like it was wrapped up tight by a boa constrictor. I leaned over the side of the bed, head between my legs and the book stared up at me.

With shaking hands, I grabbed it and pulled it under the covers with me. Instantly I felt better, my throat no longer squeezing the breath out of me. I always kept a small reading light under my pillow, which I now used to read this last biography. It told an entirely different story of Captain William Kidd.

Turns out he was a privateer, not a pirate. A privateer was a legal pirate, hired by the English government. Privateers sailed around capturing real pirate ships and gave the recovered treasure to the government.

In the late 17th century, Captain Kidd was given permission to do just that. It seemed he tried to follow his privateering orders. Only his crew forced him to attack a few ships illegally, but he made them give back the loot they stole. What kind of pirate gives back the stuff he steals? Either a really lousy one or a guy who never was a pirate.

Captain Kidd was too smart to be a lousy pirate, so I was betting that he never really wanted to be one in the first place. He did hit one of his crewmen on the head with a bucket, and that man died the next day. I wasn't justifying killing a man, but the crewman was threatening mutiny, so Kidd probably hit him in self-defense.

Seemed to me the famous pirate (non-pirate) was as misunderstood as a 13-year-old boy with the same first name. He followed orders, tried to do the right thing, but ended up with the short end of the stick. He was sentenced to death, thrown into the infamous Newgate Prison in London, and executed by hanging in 1701.

The first rope they tried to hang Kidd with broke, which was usually considered a sign from God that the accused was innocent. When I read that part, I felt a pull on my own neck. With a hand to my throbbing throat, I continued reading. Instead of letting him go, they strung him back up and hung him for real.

My breath caught and swallowing was like trying to force a full-sized steak down my throat. I had to get a drink of water before I finished the book, and even then it felt like the ghost of a noose was tugging on my neck.

After learning all this, I still didn't have any clue about where any pirate treasure was. The books hardly even mentioned Long Island Sound where Pirate Island is, and they didn't mention the island at all.

I tried explaining all of this to Andy when we met at his house on Saturday morning. His response was pretty much what I had expected it to be. "I don't care about all that historical stuff. Where do we find Kidd's treasure?"

"You don't care! What's wrong with you?" My throat tightened as I thought about Captain Kidd's—William's—death. "He shouldn't have been hanged. He was innocent, mostly." There was the matter of the death by bucket, which I maintained was an accident (a homicide at worst), not murder, which he was found guilty of along with the piracy. "How could you not care?"

"I just don't." Andy was looking at me like I had slugs in my hair, another thing that once actually happened, another among the long list of crazy things we'd done. "It was a long time ago. I care about the riches. Where is the treasure?"

Andy was the showman, all about the act. I was the groupie, not allowed to care about anything that wasn't revealed to me on stage. "I don't know," I admitted.

"What do you mean you don't know? What about all those books you read?"

I rubbed my bare feet through the stained carpet and stared at my toes. "They're mostly about Captain Kidd's life and where he got all his treasures. They don't really talk about where he buried them. Well, except for this one stash he hid on Gardiners Island off Long Island, but that was discovered before Captain Kidd died. I don't think anyone really knows where the rest of his loot is. There may not be any buried treasure."

Andy slapped his hands in frustration. "Damn."

I decided I needed more local information, like the articles Andy had shown me. "Did your mom send you anything else with the picture?"

"She just wrote a note on the back."

"Can I read it?"

Andy didn't say anything, but his face turned all red and he stared out the window, finally saying, "I don't think so. It probably won't help us find anything."

I knew better than to try to change his mind.

"My dad might have something," he said. "Wait here. I'll be back in a couple of minutes."

He left and slammed the door behind him. I noticed the photo of Pirate Island on Andy's desk. I reached to pick it up but immediately pulled away. Fingers twitching almost of their own accord, my hand snatched it up and turned it over. Before I knew what I was doing, I read the note on the back from Andy's mom.

To My Sweet Baby,

I know I don't have to tell you how much I miss you. It was such a treat to have you all to myself for those two weeks last month. I found this old photo in a book the other day and it made me think of you. Your father and I may not be married anymore, but we did have some wonderful times together. One night we found our very own treasure on Pirate Island. Maybe someday you'll find treasure there too.

Love Always,

Mommy xoxo

I could see why Andy didn't want me to read it. Not that I would have made fun of him for it. There are some things you don't tease a guy about.

The strange thing was in that moment I had picked up the photo, it was like someone else had control of my hand. I stared in disbelief at the hand holding the photo. I should have seen it as a sign of the much larger possession to come.

(I would find out William Kidd—not William Bonny—was to blame, but right then I only blamed myself, who was still just Billy.)

Guilt squeezed my stomach, and I set the photo back on the desk, note side down.

Not a minute later, Andy came back into the room. "My dad has a bunch of files in the storage area that might help us."

More reading...which had become a dangerous thing. I wondered if I could get Andy to admit on his own about his mom finding treasure on Pirate Island. The note was concrete evidence the treasure existed, but I absolutely could not ask him about it. One-hundred percent off limits.

For Billy anyway, but William Kidd didn't have such boundaries. Kidd couldn't even manage to stay in his own century, but I'm jumping ahead of myself.

Chapter 6

Back on the beach while I wait for Kristina and her boyfriend to show up for the adventure of a lifetime, I pick up a pile of sand and let the tiny pieces flow through my fingers. The briny scent of an approaching low tide tickles my nose and stirs a deep emotion inside of me, or rather inside of Kidd.

He recalls the long, arduous days at sea and the lonely rock of his ships, the *Adventure Galley* and the *Quedagh Merchant*, at night. He misses Sarah, his wife, and wonders how she and their daughters are faring in the afterlife. As a ghost, Kidd hasn't been able to reunite with his dead loved ones. A feeling of longing washes over us, greater than the many fathoms of the deepest ocean, an emotion I don't fully understand but feel all the same.

That's when I hear my former best friend say, "Billy?" It's hesitant, uncertain, not at all like the Andy I know.

"It's William," I say in a throaty voice that doesn't feel entirely my own.

He stands at the water's edge, silhouetted in the soon-to-be setting sun. "Oh, right. I forgot. William then."

"What are you doing here, Andy?"

He takes a step closer, further blocking out the sun, so I can now make out his features. His mouth is puckered in seriousness, but his eyes are wide with excitement. "I'm here to find Kidd's treasure."

I pitch a rock into the Sound at hearing that name (mine, ours?) come out of Andy's mouth. "It's not yours to find. It's ours." He shoots me a questioning look as he has no idea about my ties to Kidd and no one else is on the beach with us. "The treasure is mine," I correct myself.

I squash the handful of sand, sending the grains shooting in all directions. He turns back to all-confident Andy as he straightens up to his full height, high above my sitting body. "I'm the one who started this. My mom told me about the treasure. My dad had the information to show us where it is."

Though that's not entirely true, I have to give him some credit. He did start this whole thing, and his mom was the one who told us about the treasure, but we didn't find its location based on what we found that day in his dad's basement. That was more smoke and mirrors.

Chapter 7

At Andy's condo two weeks earlier, I tried to figure out a way to talk to Andy about his mom without revealing I had read the note. I followed him to the storage area, which was a giant shared basement for all the condos in the block. The space looked like it hadn't been vacuumed or dusted since Captain Kidd had been alive. Water stains marked the walls and cobwebs decorated the old light bulbs and pull chains that hung from the low ceiling. We made our way across the floor as a hot-water heater kicked on. I jumped.

Andy snickered. "Scared of the dark?"

"Shut up," I said. "Where's your dad's stuff?"

"Over here." He pointed to a rusted filing cabinet in the corner. The hinges squeaked as he opened the top drawer. He pulled out a bunch of files. There were all kinds of electronic manuals, piles of old bills and receipts, and even a wrinkled book report of Andy's with a big C+ written at the top.

He handed over a folder with a bunch of newspaper clippings about Pirate Island. I looked over one of the articles, careful not to tear the delicate paper. Most of them were similar to the ones Andy had shown me at the library. A few were about different incidences that had happened there. One was from 1986 and was about a group of teenagers who had almost burned down the whole island with their campfire.

Andy flipped through a small paperback. "Oooh. Listen to this." He read from the book. "'It being said that the notorious Kidd buried money on the south side of it, beside a rock, two or three persons went privately, on a moon light night, to dig for it. After much preparatory ceremony, such as drawing a circle round the rock, and reciting some words of in…incan…'"

I looked over Andy's shoulder and found the word he was trying to sound out. "Incantation."

"Whatever." He continued reading, "'They began to dig, and so far succeeded as to hit the lid of an iron box, when looking up into the air, they saw coming down direct upon them the figure of a man without a head. They dropped their spades, and ran as most others would have done, and escaped.'

"Idiots," Andy interrupted himself. "I would've grabbed the box."

"Keep reading," I said.

"Okay, okay," he said. "'Looking toward the spot they saw it enveloped in smoke and blue flame. Returning to the island the next day, their spades had disappeared, they found the ground smooth, and no traces left of its having been dug.'"

"How did they know the ghost was Captain Kidd if it had no head? It could have been the ghost of one of the Native Americans who once lived on the island or the ghost of a guest at the old resort."

"Who cares?" Andy never gave me any credit when I had a good point. "Now we know where the treasure is: on the south side of the island by a big rock. We've gotta go there and check it out. I have a game tomorrow morning. Maybe we can go after that."

"We don't have a boat," I pointed out. "We have to wait until we can walk out."

A minor problem like that wasn't likely to stop him. "So we'll find out when low tide is."

"And it's illegal to go on the island." My second good point in as many minutes.

"I already told you, we're a couple of kids exploring. No one's going to care."

I fell in line, captive audience eager for a show, and we headed back to his room to start up his computer. The low tides for Sunday were 7:47 a.m. and 8:21 p.m. The morning was out because of Andy's game. Sunset was at 7:54, which meant we'd be walking out to Pirate Island in the dark. I wasn't exactly thrilled about that, but I didn't dare say anything.

It wasn't that I was scared, or at least that was what I

told myself. I thought it might be easier to find the spot where the treasure was hidden in the light of day. Plus, in order for the whole plan to work, I had to convince my mom to let me sleep at Andy's. He was always welcome to stay at our house, but I hadn't been allowed to sleep at his since he had moved. I overheard my mom tell my dad that the condo was in a bad neighborhood. Was that enough of an excuse to get out of this? Did I want to get out of it?

Thoughts of Captain Kidd swelled up in me. Trekking to a small island in the dark would not have made it on to his list of fears. Suddenly I felt a little braver.

Chapter 8

Later that night while my mom made dinner, I tried to convince her to let me go to the sleepover. "But, Mom, I wanna stay at Andy's."

"Why can't you stay here?" she asked.

My mouth moved without my permission. "Andy just got a new video game. I don't have the right game console."

Lie and lie. Andy did not have a new video game, and I had all the newest game consoles. Yet my mom stopped chopping to actually look at my eager face.

"Will Andy's father be home? Can he pick you up? Your father and I won't be home until late tomorrow night."

"Yes." Another lie. I planned on riding my bike to the beach and meeting Andy there.

My mom rubbed her temples. "Okay, but you have to promise to stay inside after dark. Okay?"

I managed to keep a straight face while a fourth lie crossed my lips. "I promise." I gave her a hug, my arms feeling bigger than the actual skinny ones wrapped around her torso. "Thanks, Mom."

She went back to her chopping. "Your father and I are meeting with clients tomorrow. We're leaving very early in the morning."

I rummaged in the refrigerator for a snack, despite the slight pit in my stomach. Seemed like the only time I had seen my father all summer was when we'd taken a trip to the beach last month.

My mom appeared behind me and opened the refrigerator door wider, reaching around me to select a peach from the crisper. "Here. Eat this. I just bought it at the farmer's market."

I spotted a cheese stick and pulled it out of the drawer. She grabbed it and tossed it back in, shutting the door with me practically in the fridge. She slapped the peach into my hand. "Dinner will be ready in a half hour. I don't need you ruining your appetite."

I slumped into a chair at the kitchen table and bit into the fruit. The sweet, sticky juice squirted down my chin with a loud squelch. "So you and Dad have to work on Sunday again," I complained between bites.

She handed me a napkin and pulled a pot out of the cabinet. "Yes. You know your father is working on a big class-action case. We need signatures, and the weekend is the best time to get them." She pursed her lips, and I knew I wasn't going to like what she said next. "Kristina's in charge while we're gone."

"Why does she get to be in charge?" I asked,

accidentally spitting a piece of peach on the table. "I'm thirteen years old. It's not like I need a baby-sitter."

"Manners, Billy. Don't talk with your mouth full." She grabbed a rag and wiped my mess. "Kris is just keeping an eye on everything."

"Aren't I old enough to look after myself?" I whined. "She is so mean when you're not around."

"I'm sure she'll be fine. Your sister's in charge tomorrow. This isn't up for debate."

I pouted until my mom said she'd tell Kristina to be nice. Then she ran her fingers through my dark brown hair. "Please be good tomorrow. Okay?"

I crossed my arms over my chest. "Fine."

I'd put up with my sister for the day, but only because my mom was letting me stay at Andy's. I was almost excited to check out Pirate Island, even if it was going to be dark out. I had a new-found sense of adventure.

Chapter 9

After dinner, I needed to pack for the next night's trip to Pirate Island. I made a list before I went in search of everything. My dad's big flashlight was out in the garage with his tool belt. There was also an old pocketknife in one of the compartments. I slipped it into my pocket...just in case.

My dad would never notice his stuff was missing. He probably hadn't touched any of his tools since he'd started that still unfinished tree house on my sixth birthday.

Back in my room, I found my old hiking boots in the closet. I had read that Pirate Island was infested with giant rats, and boots would offer more protection than sneakers or sandals. Andy had wanted to get one of those metal detectors—like you always see old people with on the beach —but we didn't know anyone who had one. We'd have to rely on our eyes for clues.

Before I went to bed, I read through more of the information we had found in Andy's basement. It said that it was a common belief that the treasure could only be dug up by three people—no more, no less. We'd have to work on finding a third treasure hunter.

I also started rereading the biography on Captain Kidd to see if I had missed anything. I could picture him standing at the wheel of the *Adventure Galley*—the coolest name for a ship I could've imagined. His hair blowing in the wind, and his coat billowing out behind him. Shouting orders at his crew, and taking no back talk from anyone.

Seemed all I did was take orders. Andy ordering me around whenever we hung out. My mom making me eat healthy food and putting my sister in charge. Kristina thinking it was okay to boss me around. Though I wouldn't have minded if my dad hassled me a bit more; it would mean he was actually around.

Maybe I needed to act more like Captain Kidd and give out orders. Just as long as I didn't end up like him— with a noose around my neck. I shuddered when I pictured him hanging from the gallows. My flesh prickled at the thought of his rotting corpse that was left on display along the River Thames for three years as a warning to other pirates.

He wasn't even a pirate! He was a privateer, working for the same government who executed him. My anger over it all made it hard to fall asleep. I huddled deep under my covers with my flashlight and Kidd's biography, soaking in the words like a towel absorbing water.

When my eyes finally got too tired to read, I lay in the

dark, thinking about the ghost of Captain Kidd. I dreamed that Andy and I were digging alongside a hooded figure. It was midnight, and the moon was full. A rat crawled across my boots and one scampered over Andy's sneakers. I screamed as dozens of rats darted out of the shadows. The headless body of Captain Kidd swooped down on us—even headless I recognized the figure as his. Its blue light engulfed the island, chasing us as we ran back across the sandbar. I didn't exactly get a great night of sleep.

Even worse, a shriek startled me awake the next morning. I hurried down the hallway past my sister's bedroom. The door was open and no one was there. No one was in the living room or kitchen either. Another shriek led me to the back window. Kristina was sitting on the deck, her feet dangling in the pool. Someone was in the water, tickling her legs, all but his arms blocked by Kristina's body.

I walked out the back sliding doors onto the deck. "Hey! What's going on?"

"Oh! Hey, Billy," my sister said.

"What are you doing?" I rubbed goose bumps off my arms.

"Swimming."

The guy in the pool leaned around Kris and smiled. His hair was bright orange.

"Hey, I'm Justin," he said. "Tina's boyfriend."

"Tina?" I asked.

Kristina flipped her natural, dark brown hair and giggled. "Oh, that's just what Justin calls me. He thinks it sounds more punk rock."

"I'm in a band," Justin said as if that made it okay for him to call my sister Tina.

"Kris," I said, emphasizing how much it didn't sound like Tina. "You know you're not supposed to have boys here when Mom's not around."

"So, Mom doesn't have to know."

I folded my arms across my chest and pressed my lips together in a frown. Kristina jumped onto the deck and headed towards me. "C'mon. You don't have to tell Mom. Do you?"

I kept silent. Usually a situation like this played out where I would say "no" and Kristina would pound on me until I agreed. I decided I wasn't going to take orders from her anymore. I slipped back through the sliding doors into the kitchen, slamming it shut in her face. I flipped the lock and put the wooden rod in place for good measure.

She tapped on the glass. "Don't make me come in the front door."

"I'll lock that, too!" I shouted.

She knew I could easily get through the house to the front door before she could get off the deck and around the house.

She crossed her arms and tapped her bare foot on the deck. "Listen, I'll make it up to you. What do you want?"

she asked through the closed doors.

I thought for a minute. Kristina didn't make offers like that very often.

"I want you to help me find Captain Kidd's treasure," I finally said.

"What are you talking about?"

"Andy and I are looking for Captain Kidd's lost treasure," I said a little louder to make sure she heard me through the glass. "We think it's buried on Pirate Island."

She rolled her eyes.

"Fine," I said, making like I was heading for the phone. "I'll go call Mom now."

She threw her hands up and shouted, "Alright! I'll help. Just keep your mouth shut."

I made a motion of locking my mouth and throwing away the key. Giving out orders seemed to be working; we now had our third treasure hunter. Maybe I'd have to act like Captain Kidd more often. (Very soon I would be doing much more than *acting* like him.)

Chapter 10

Instead of hanging around with Kristina and her boyfriend all day, I walked to the library. I stacked all the books on the return desk, but at the last minute, snatched my favorite biography back up. Something beyond my understanding compelled me to keep it.

The same librarian who had looked up my library card stood at the counter. She saw the stack of books and winked. "How very prompt of you, William Bonny."

It was a little weird she had remembered my name, but I smiled at the sound of it. William sounded so much better than Billy.

"Do you have a section on local history?" I asked her. I wanted to learn as much as possible about Pirate Island before nightfall...when I would be on it!

Her eyes crinkled at the edges, and she broke into a soft smile. "Of course. Follow me." She led me to a quiet corner of the library and pointed to the bottom shelf. "This is where we keep all the local resources. Come and find me if you need help locating anything specific."

Before she reached the end of the aisle, I settled on the floor to skim the titles. Most of them looked pretty boring, even for a reader like me. I pulled out one about ghost stories of New England and another on legends and myths of Long Island Sound.

An hour passed and I hadn't discovered anything that would help me find Captain Kidd's treasure. I did find one story about him, but it had to do with Gardiners Island, which I already knew about. Before Captain Kidd was executed, he went back to the U.S. and buried treasure on Gardiners Island in Long Island Sound. It was dug up and used against him in his trial. I had tried to tell Andy about it, but he hadn't listened. He sometimes pulled his own smoke-and-mirrors routine on himself. I grabbed the biography from my backpack, checked the index for Gardiners Island, and flipped through to the right pages. Like the last time I read that section, it felt like I was living it rather than reading it. The details of Captain Kidd's life sprang from the pages. I could almost smell the sea and taste the salt on my lips.

Then I got to the text of an actual letter written by Captain Kidd. Its old-fashioned language had confused me the first time I'd seen it.

> *...in my late proceedings in the Indies I have lodged goods and Tresure to the value of one hundred thousand pounds, which I desire the Government may have the benefitt of, in order thereto, I shall*

desire no manner of liberty but to be kept prisoner on board such shipp as may be appointed for that purpose, and only give the necessary directions and in case I faile therin I desire no favour but to be forthwith Executed acording to my Sentence.

I was trying to puzzle out what Captain Kidd meant when a voice made me jump in surprise. "Can I help you with something?"

A man stood over me, smiling. His shiny black hair was tied up at the base of his neck and covered on top with a red bandanna. His face and arms were a deep hue, like he spent a lot of time on a boat or at the beach. He was dressed nice enough in a button-down shirt and khaki pants, but I knew better than to talk to strangers, even well-dressed ones.

"No, thank you," I said as I stood.

I started to walk away when the man's hand touched my shoulder.

"You sure?" he asked. "I might be able to help you find something."

This guy was really creeping me out. What was he going to do next, ask me if I wanted some candy? Then I noticed the words on the pocket of his shirt "Library Staff" and written under that the name "Ken." Okay, so maybe this guy could help me after all.

I showed him the page with the letter. "Do you know what this means?"

His eyes darted from side to side as he read the passage. "It seems this person claimed that he hid treasure somewhere. Treasure worth one-hundred thousand pounds. Pounds are British money." I nodded because I already knew that. "He seemed to be in some sort of trouble and was offering to give the money to the government in exchange for help. But it says they ignored his letter."

"So the treasure could still be out there."

"Maybe. If you believe this person was telling the truth." Keeping his place in the book with his finger, he flipped it shut and glanced at the front cover.

I believed Captain Kidd was telling the truth. It was his last effort to try and save his neck. Thinking about the hanging brought a tingling to my own neck, and I rubbed it self-consciously.

"Hmmm," was all Ken said as he handed back the book.

I thanked him and returned the books to the shelf. Tucking the biography under my arm, I headed back home, sweating in the heat of the afternoon sun. The humidity sucked all the water from my mouth; it was drier than Death Valley. I imagined sucking on an ice-cold popsicle, sticky juices running down my chin.

When I reached the duck pond behind city hall, I stopped at the edge and stared at the water. My tongue was a giant cotton ball. The green algae floating on the surface and the duck poop under my feet banished all thoughts of drinking the water. I ran the rest of the way home, dreaming about the ride in the water park where you float in a tube down the river, waterfalls drenching your head and jets shooting at you.

I ran straight through the house and into the kitchen where I drank practically a gallon of water right from the tap.

Kristina was watching TV in the living room. Thankfully her boyfriend had left. I didn't want to eat dinner with the two of them, but I didn't want to eat alone either. The strange sensations I'd been having when thinking about Kidd had me kind of freaked out, or maybe it was the thought of going to Pirate Island in a few hours.

We ordered pizza and had it delivered. The humidity broke a little as evening approached, so we ate on the deck by the pool. We laughed and joked around with each other. It was a lot of fun, like before Kristina started high school. I almost didn't want to leave, but I couldn't ignore the part of me (the part that was already connected to Kidd) that yearned to explore Pirate Island.

Chapter 11

The sun and I were racing. I pedaled my bike hard, asphalt passing by at breakneck speed. My house was about two miles from Long Island Sound, and it was another mile or so to the beach with the sandbar. The sun dipped low, and I pedaled harder. Unfortunately, the sun won. No one was in sight when I reached the boardwalk. I locked my bike to the base of one of those sightseeing binoculars.

A cool breeze dried the sweat on my neck and raised goose bumps on my bare arms and legs. I guess I was going to have to get used to having goose bumps all the time, at least until we found the treasure or until Andy got bored with searching. I retrieved my dad's flashlight from my backpack. Even with the light, it was hard to see how far the tide had receded, but the sandbar looked pretty exposed.

I clicked off the flashlight, not wanting to waste the batteries. There was no moon in the sky. I was glad for light pollution. To the west, the lights from a small airport and the beacon of a distant lighthouse provided a little brightness. To the east, the lights of the harbor and the street lamps followed the coastline. Out on the water, the red and green beams of boats bobbed up and down with the waves. Pirate Island's silhouette loomed against the sky, not a light on it.

I expected Andy to sneak up on me because he always did things like that, but the minutes ticked away and he didn't come.

The smell of low tide twisted my stomach. The constant waves reminded me of the passing time. My light-up watch showed it was 8:20 already. Low tide was in one minute. Where was Andy? If he didn't get here soon, we wouldn't have any time to explore. The tide wouldn't take long to come in. I didn't exactly want to spend all night stuck on Pirate Island. Not to mention my mom would have a fit if she found out where I was.

I skipped rocks to pass the time. I couldn't see that well, but I could hear them skimming off the water. Splish, splish, splish, splish, splish, splish, splish. Seven! All right!

The sound of tires sliding on a sandy surface announced Andy's arrival. In the light of a streetlamp, I watched him throw his bike down, not even bothering to lock it up. He ran over, but I wasn't feeling so enthusiastic anymore. It was 8:35. Leave it to Andy to be late to his own treasure hunt. Leave it to him to let me sit alone in the dark waiting. Leave it to him to show up like he didn't care about any of it.

"What're we waiting for?" he asked with a grin.

I shrugged. I told myself to be like Captain Kidd. Don't take orders from anyone, make my own orders.

"C'mon." Andy grabbed my arm.

I pulled away. "You're late."

"So what?"

I folded my arms across my chest. I wanted to yell at him for being inconsiderate. He always did this kind of thing to me, but I never called him out.

"I'm sorry, alright," he said. He sounded pretty sincere. "My mom called. She didn't want to let me get off the phone. You know how she can be."

Any other excuse wouldn't have cut it with me. Like I said before, my best friend knows how to get what he wants.

But there was something else, too. A prickling sensation telling me to walk out to the island, that it was important. That feeling, more than Andy, convinced me.

"Fine," I said. "Let's get this treasure hunt started."

I kept the flashlight pointed at the ground in front of our feet. Shells and sand crunched as we walked over the sandbar. Andy was jabbering on about his game—they had won—and I half listened. My ears were alert for any unusual sounds. Luckily the tide was pretty low and the middle section of the sandbar was wide. It didn't take long for us to reach the island.

The wind was strong. Andy's golden locks blew all around his face. I wondered what he would do if I called him Goldilocks. Was he ever going to cut it? Did girls—Ella Platt—really like long hair? A squawk distracted me.

Andy jumped this time. A flash of white, contrasted against the dark sky, flew out of the trees. It was just a bird.

I laughed. "Scared?"

"Yeah right," Andy said. "Let's try and find the rock. Where's the south side of the island?"

"Around the other side of the trees." I flashed the light in that direction to find a temporary beach fence enclosing most of the interior of the island. Big "No Trespassing" signs hung from the fence. Trees and brush blocked the light from revealing any more secrets beyond the fence.

We walked around the perimeter. There were lots of rocks and many of them were slick with algae. Sure-footed Andy took each step with confidence. I was a bit more cautious. A motorboat whirred by, and I whipped my head towards the sound. My boot slipped into the water, soaking my foot up to the ankle. I let out a yelp.

"Shhh," Andy hissed. "I think I hear something." He stopped, his feet balanced on two different rocks.

"It's probably just a boat," I whispered.

My left foot was submerged in the water. Being on Pirate Island made me want to keep my voice low and my head down. I reminded myself that Captain Kidd probably hadn't been scared when (if?) he buried his treasure on the island. Was I really starting to believe the loot was actually here?

"No," Andy whispered back. "I think it's something else."

"I don't hear anything. Can we keep moving?" My foot was colder than a pint of ice cream surrounded by ice cubes inside a deep freezer.

It wasn't long before we turned a corner and the flashlight illuminated a large rock that was a good four-feet high and wider than I was tall. The only problem was there was a similar boulder about ten feet from the first one. And a third one, closer to the trees.

"Which is the right one?" Andy asked, forgetting or not caring to whisper.

I shrugged, though he probably couldn't see me. How was I supposed to know? But it was a good question. We couldn't exactly go making holes all over the island without bringing too much attention to ourselves.

A white light engulfed us. I shielded my eyes, but I couldn't see a single thing besides blinding brightness. For a second, I thought it was Captain Kidd's ghost.

"Run!" yelled Andy.

Water splashed up as he rushed by. I turned my back on the light. Andy was running back to the sandbar. I charged after him, trying my best not to fall. Both my feet were soaked right through my boots. The light followed us.

"Stop! This is the U.S. Coast Guard!" a voice called over a megaphone.

The U.S. Coast Guard! We were in big trouble. I generally listen to authority figures, but this time I kept running. My backpack bounced up and down. I gripped my dad's flashlight so hard my knuckles hurt. My legs felt like they were bigger than ever before, like I was man-sized—pirate-sized. I ran so fast I caught up with quick-footed Andy, my lungs barely burning with exertion.

We sprinted back across the sandbar. The light wasn't shining on us anymore, but we kept moving. A stitch burned my side. I reached the bikes first. I fumbled with the lock. The Coast Guard's boat rumbled not far from shore. Andy grabbed his bike and grunted. We were both too winded to talk, but I understood. I jumped on the foot pegs, and we rode away from the beach.

Chapter 12

We were at the park a block away from Andy's house when he dropped his bike. I fell off the pegs and landed in the grass. Laughing hysterically, he rolled onto his back.

When he caught his breath, he stood up and pumped his fist into the air. "Wooo! That was awesome!"

Awesome wasn't the word that came to mind, more like terrifying. The Captain Kidd braveness from before seemed to elude me at the moment (our connection wasn't as strong as it is now). "Yeah. That was great."

"I can't believe the Coast Guard showed up." Andy danced around in a circle.

I remained on the ground, afraid my legs would shake if I tried to stand up. "We could've gotten in serious trouble. We were trespassing on state property."

"It was still awesome. And we didn't get caught, so no big deal, right?"

"I guess." Easy for him to say, he didn't need a long-dead pirate to make him fearless. "We have to go back and get my bike."

I had told my mom that Andy's dad could bring my bike to their condo for me. She was expecting me to have it with me tomorrow morning when she picked me up. Coast Guard or not, I had to get it back tonight.

"I don't wanna ride all the way back to the beach," Andy whined. "Can't you get it tomorrow or something?"

"No. I'm not leaving my bike there all night. My parents will kill me if they find out where we've been."

It took some convincing, but Andy finally gave me a ride back to the beach. Luckily, there was no sign of the Coast Guard. I pedaled as hard as I could to keep up with Andy on the way to his condo.

That night as I lay in my sleeping bag on Andy's floor, I went over in my head everything that had happened. I knew we needed a more specific treasure location. The question was how to find it.

I dreamed about Captain Kidd's ghost again. He had a head this time but no body. It hovered in the air, laughing at us, while we dug holes all over Pirate Island.

* * * *

For the next two days all I thought about was how to find the treasure. I reread the articles and Captain Kidd's biography, I looked up Pirate Island on the Internet, and I read the little paperback book from Andy's basement so many times I practically memorized it. They gave me nothing new, no flash of brilliance to set me on a new course for the treasure.

My connection to Kidd dried up as well. I hadn't felt so much as a twinge in my neck, and all the courage I'd gained had vanished along with the Coast Guard.

Though my spiritual connection with Kidd was gone, I remained obsessed with the treasure and the non-pirate who buried it. The more I thought about him, the more I was convinced he was wrongly accused of piracy. He hadn't deserved to be executed, even taking into account the crewman he hit with the bucket. It was self-defense, not murder.

The circumstances of the broken rope really bothered me. Usually a rope breaking would be taken as a sign of God, and the accused would be allowed to live. But that was not the fate of poor Kidd. Nope, they strung him up again and killed him. He had good reason to haunt this world as a ghost, maybe even on Pirate Island.

Or maybe he was doing his haunting by possessing people to use their bodies to get revenge. (As I now suspect is the case with me, despite the lack of connection I was experiencing at the time.) Not knowing where the desire came from, I believed if I could find the treasure, Kidd's spirit would be able to rest.

Chapter 13

Andy had double practices all week long, so he wasn't able to help with any more research on exactly where the treasure was hidden. Somehow he had managed to get permission to skip our writing class that week, too. Normally I loved class, but that week I suffered through it alone.

While I was supposed to be writing a paragraph based on the prompt on the board, I pulled out the book about Pirate Island and slipped it onto my lap. I skimmed through all the historical stuff until I found the page with the story of the people who had almost found the loot. If Andy and I could find these people and talk to them, maybe they could help us. Their names weren't mentioned, so the question remained how to find out who they were.

I reread the passage, searching for any clues.

A voice startled me. "Mr. Bonny."

I hate it when people use my last name. Someone always points out how it's a girl's name.

Worse than the name, though, was the person who

was saying it: Mrs. Shields. She stood behind me with a clear view of the book. It was usually Andy who got in trouble for this kind of thing.

"What are you doing?" she demanded.

My face heated up. "I umm...I'm sorry."

Lips pursed, she held out an open palm. "Hand it over."

"No." The word burst out without my permission and hung there in the room for everyone to stare at. Nope, that was me they were gawking at. My neck tingled, and I had a feeling I wasn't totally in control of my own body. What was wrong with me? (I was doing a pretty good job with the smoke-and-mirrors act, being in denial about Kidd's connection to me.)

I fixed my gaze on the table and turned over the contraband. A couple of girls giggled, and I was sure Ella's tinkly voice was among them.

"All right," Mrs. Shields said. "Quiet down. Back to the prompt."

She sat down at her desk. I tried really hard to concentrate on writing, but my pen didn't move an inch on my paper. I watched Mrs. Shields flip through the book. I forced myself to look back at the writing prompt. My face burned hotter than a flaming hoop at a circus act, and I was the one-man show. *Step up, see the amazing Billy embarrass himself.*

Fifteen agonizing minutes passed before Mrs. Shields

announced class was over. "Don't forget next week is our second-to-last class of the summer, so have your submission pieces ready for our literary journal."

As part of the class, everyone had to submit one polished piece of writing to be included in a printed-out journal. Mrs. Shields was putting the whole thing together and needed to have them in time to make copies. If I survived until next week—and by the look on Mrs. Shields's face as she turned her attention to me, I doubted I would—I had a few finishing touches to put on my ghost story before it would be ready.

I grabbed my stuff, shoved it in my bag, and headed for the door.

"Billy," Mrs. Shields said. "Please come here a minute."

Uh oh! I looked at my shoes, at the board, out the open doorway, at anything but my teacher. All the same, her eyes burned a hole into my already flaming head.

"I normally catch my students writing notes or sending text messages during class. Not reading books on local history. I know you're here voluntarily, but I still expect my students to stay on task. Is this part of a summer assignment for one of your fall classes?"

"Not exactly," I managed to say. It didn't escape my attention that she was focusing on the book and not my reaction. A small miracle.

"Well, what is it for then?" she asked.

I kept my lips sealed tight, like when I had made the promise to Kristina and locked up my mouth and threw away the key.

"Billy," said Mrs. Shields. "You can tell me. Maybe I can help."

It was the same thing Ken, the man in the library, had said. It seemed everyone but the one person I wanted help from was offering it.

She held up the book. "What is this about?"

I scuffed the soles of my shoes on the floor and shrugged. Mrs. Shields waited silently. I drew a deep breath and pulled in a gulp of oxygen, hoping it would inject me with some courage. Captain Kidd had been brave; I could be brave too.

I looked her straight in the eye. "It was an idea we had, Andy and me. We want to find Captain William Kidd's treasure. He was supposed to have all these riches on his ship, but most of them were never found."

"Yes. I've heard of Captain Kidd and his missing treasure. I also know you're not supposed to go on Pirate Island."

I was careful how I worded what I was about to say. "What else do you know about Pirate Island?"

She laughed, a much younger sound than I thought could possibly come from her mouth. "The legends about Pirate Island go way back before *I* was born. You live in this town long enough, you hear some pretty amazing stories."

I was a little afraid to ask, but if she knew something about Pirate Island that could help in the search, I had to find out. "Have you ever heard a story about people who were looking for the treasure and were scared away by Kidd's ghost?"

She smiled. "I've heard a few stories like that." Then her face turned serious. "I'm not sure how true most of them are."

"Do you think there's treasure on Pirate Island?"

"No one's ever found much, but I suppose there's always a chance."

I thought of the note from Andy's mom. How she claimed to have found treasure there. I still hadn't figured out a way to bring that up with Andy. Another question occurred to me, but it seemed a bit silly.

As if reading my mind, Mrs. Shields said, "Billy, is there anything else?"

I (Kidd?) went for it. "Have you ever looked for Captain Kidd's treasure?"

She blushed, and then her eyes turned all dreamy-like. "A long time ago my friends and I spent a night on Pirate Island. It was when we were in high school. I probably shouldn't even be telling you this."

She giggled again, sounding more like my sister than a teacher. "Later we told our parents we got stuck when the tide came in. But we had planned it all along, even brought sleeping bags with us. We built a fire and talked and laughed for hours. Eventually everyone fell asleep, except for me. I wasn't tired. The island had a certain energy about it that kept me awake."

I wondered if this was the moment when I would discover the exact location of the treasure.

"I walked down to the water and looked at the stars for a long time," Mrs. Shields continued. "Then I heard a noise. I thought it was one of my friends coming to look for me. When I turned around, no one was there. Then I heard the noise again. It was louder this time. It sounded like moaning. I thought maybe someone was hurt, so I walked around the island, searching for whatever it was."

It was beyond weird trying to imagine Mrs. Shields as a teenager, never mind trying to picture her wandering around Pirate Island alone in the dark. Then she laughed again and sounded so much like a teen.

"Well I never found anything. Eventually I went back to my friends and fell asleep. I never told anyone about it, but it made me wonder about Pirate Island. For such a small piece of land, it has a very long history."

A car honked outside. Mrs. Shields looked out the window with a startled face. "Oh. I'm sorry I've kept you so long."

I told her it was okay and headed for the door, my mind churning.

"Billy," she said. "People often exaggerate when telling stories. Not everything they say is true. It's like your ghost story. Parts may be inspired by real people, but there aren't really ghosts in your best friend's attic, right?"

I nodded, not sure what I believed anymore.

"Promise me you won't do anything unsafe or illegal," she said.

I promised I wouldn't, knowing full well I had already done something illegal. I couldn't get over Mrs. Shields being young and spending the night on Pirate Island. That island definitely had the power to bring out the stranger side of people. And things were just going to keep getting stranger.

Chapter 14

Even with Mrs. Shields's confession about her night on Pirate Island, I still had no way of knowing where Kidd's treasure was hidden. That afternoon, for what felt like the millionth time, I studied all the materials I had gathered. In particular, I focused on a hand-drawn picture of the island in the paperback and a real map of it I had found on the Internet. Pirate Island was only 14 acres. How could it be so hard to find the location of the loot in such a small space?

I decided to talk to my sister. She had promised she would help and had done nothing so far. Kristina was in her room with her headphones on when I knocked on the open door. I clutched the paperback book in my hands. Swiveling her desk chair away from the door, she ignored me.

"Kris," I said. "Will you listen to me for a sec."

She kept her back to me and hummed loudly. I banged hard on the doorframe. "Kristina! You promised you'd help me!"

She continued to ignore me. I decided to take more

drastic measures. "I'll have to tell Mom and Dad that your boyfriend was—"

She grabbed me by the arm with one hand and put her other hand over my mouth. I licked it, and she punched me in the stomach. While I lay on the ground, she slammed the door and threw her headphones on the bed.

She towered above me. "What do you think you're doing?"

I managed to stand up. "You said you'd help us."

"So."

"So, I need help figuring something out."

Kris's cell phone rang. She answered it and began chatting away. I flicked her arm and put up my hands. She mouthed the words "I'm busy" and lay on her bed. She was really annoying.

Summoning all my new-found courage, I said, "Fine. Ignore me. I think I'll go downstairs and have a chat with Mom."

"Melissa, hold on a sec," Kristina said. "What, Billy?"

"Andy and I are at a dead end." More like *I* was at a dead end (well, Kidd and I), but Andy was involved enough to include him. "We need help figuring out exactly where the treasure is."

"How should I know where some treasure is?"

"I don't know, but we're all out of ideas. Can't you think of something?"

Kristina stared at me for a few seconds, sighed, and

put the phone back up to her ear. "Let me call you back." Then she turned to me. "What exactly are you looking for?"

"Captain Kidd's lost treasure," I said. "I think it might be on Pirate Island."

"You're kidding, right?"

She shot me a look of annoyance and grabbed the paperback out of my hands. Flipping through it quickly, she paused occasionally to read. Then she shut it, stared at the cover a minute, and handed it back to me. She rummaged around in her desk drawer and pulled out a pamphlet. "Why don't you ask Eleanor Birch?"

"Who?" I asked.

"Eleanor Birch." She handed me the pamphlet. "She works for the historical society. She's a little...kooky, but if anyone knows about town history, it's her."

"Oh." I wasn't big on contacting strangers. "How do you know her?"

Her face turned the color of strawberry jam. "Justin took me there on our first date. She helped him set up the whole thing."

I laughed so hard my stomach hurt. "He took you to the historical society on a date. What a loser!"

Kris punched me in the arm. "Shut up! He made a picnic lunch with chocolate-covered strawberries. We ate on the lawns of the historic houses and had a view of the harbor. It was romantic."

I bent over and fake gagged. I knew it was likely to

earn me a beating, but I couldn't help it. Picturing Justin, with his orange hair, on the grounds of the historical houses having a picnic was too much to handle.

Luckily Kristina's cell phone rang, distracting her from doing any more bodily harm. "Hey, Justin. Hold on a sec." She held the phone away from her ear and asked, "Are we done here?"

"Yeah." I made a face and said in a stupid voice, "Tina."

She shoved me out of her room and slammed the door in my face. I should've been grateful; my sister had given me more help than she had in years. Still, I was kind of annoyed at being thrown out.

I had a new lead on the treasure hunt, now it was a matter of following through on it. Easier said than done.

My hands were sweating as I went into my dad's office to call this Eleanor Birch lady. I took a deep breath. Unlike Kristina, whose cell phone was practically attached to her face, I wasn't exactly a phone person. Usually I only talked to my grandmother, or maybe to Andy to make plans. Calling a complete stranger was totally different.

Pursuing Captain Kidd's treasure was forcing me into all kinds of uncomfortable situations. None of them were likely to end up as bad as it ended up for him, though. I rubbed my neck absentmindedly. I would have to suck it up and get it done.

I marked Eleanor Birch's phone number with my

finger, grabbed the phone, and punched in the numbers. It rang once...twice. Then it rang seven more times before an answering machine picked up. I clicked the end button.

Maybe I should've left a message, but I wasn't sure what to say. *Oh, hi. Thought you might be able to find the treasure of a pirate who's been dead over 300 years.* Somehow I didn't think that would work.

I jumped at the sound of the phone ringing. It was still in my hand, so it was easy for me to answer it with a quizzical, "Hello?"

"Hello?" came the voice of an old lady. "Hello?"

"Yes, hello," I said a bit louder. "Who is this?"

"Is that you, Daniel?" the voice asked.

"No." Now I was practically shouting. "My name is Billy. Who are you?"

"Did you just call me?"

"Maybe. Are you Eleanor Birch?"

"Why yes, I am. I didn't hear the phone ringing, but your number came up on the stalker I.D. thingy my neighbor got me. I thought maybe it was her son Daniel trying to call."

When Kristina had called this lady kooky, she was definitely on to something. "You mean caller I.D."

"Yes, yes. Of course. *Caller* I.D." Her voiced sounded huffy. "What did you say your name was? I'm not interested in buying anything if that's what you're calling about."

A full minute of silenced passed. I seemed to have lost

all ability to think or talk. Not very smooth at all.

"Hello?" asked Ms. Birch. "Are you still there?"

Be brave like Kidd, I told myself. And it was easier than I expected. I took a deep breath and a feeling of lightness filled me. "Oh, um…yeah. William…my name is William…Bonny."

"William" I said, like Kidd, not Billy. The pirate was pulling me in deeper without me even knowing it.

"What did you want, dearie?" the old lady asked.

I launched into a very long and wordy explanation of why I had called. I mentioned Andy and my sister, the books I had read, and even the story Mrs. Shields had told me. I tried to speak clearly, but I wasn't sure she understood everything.

"Dearie," she said when I finally stopped talking. "What did you say your name was?"

"William." It sounded so right to call myself that.

"William," she repeated. "I don't like talking about Pirate Island. It's thrice cursed. There's Kidd's curse, that Indian chief's curse, and that Spanish pirate's curse. No, no. I don't like talking about it at all."

My hopes of finding a lead were sinking faster than a ship with a hundred cannon-sized holes in its hull. "Maybe you could just tell me someone who will talk to me about Pirate Island."

"William, dearie, Pirate Island is a terrible place, only fit for rats. It'd be best to forget about that cursed place."

The phone disconnected with a quiet click. She'd sunk my pirate ship! I sat in silence until the sound of a dial tone reminded me that I hadn't clicked off the phone. My head ached. Even worse, I had hit another dead end. At this rate, we'd never get our hands on Kidd's treasure.

Chapter 15

Andy's enthusiasm for the treasure hunt had gotten us only so far. Reading had given me more questions than answers. And my sister's suggestion of contacting Eleanor Birch had pretty much been a failure. I was out of ideas. I decided to start back at the beginning: the public library.

I rode my bike there the next day. I was all sweaty when I arrived, and the cool air inside gave me the old familiar goose bumps. But at least my neck felt like just a neck.

The research section was so quiet I could hear the hum of the central air and the click-click of the librarian's keyboard. I headed right for the books on local history and found nothing new. From my backpack, I pulled out my favorite book about Kidd, which I had taken to carrying around with me at all times, along with the paperback about Pirate Island.

In the biography, there was a whole chapter on his actions before his arrest in Boston. On June 11, 1699, Kidd took his boat to drop off his lawyer in Stonington,

Connecticut. It wasn't until July 1, 1699 that the pirate-not-pirate landed in Boston, only to be arrested several days later. In those 20 days, he roamed Long Island Sound on his ship.

There was undeniable proof he hid treasure on Gardiners Island during this time, and the loot was later confiscated as evidence to be used against him in trial. If he had sailed anywhere near it, surely he would've noticed Pirate Island along the way.

There were other islands in the Sound, but lots of them were smaller than Pirate Island and grouped together in big chains. How would he be able to tell which island to come back to? He didn't have all the modern navigation tools back then, so he would have to rely on maps, which were often inaccurate.

Hardly worth it to bury treasure if he could never find it again. Pirate Island was the perfect place: distinct and memorable.

My mind raced with the probability that there was actually treasure on Pirate Island. The proof was continuing to pile up in favor of it. The problem was finding someone who knew exactly where the treasure was buried. Eleanor Birch might know, but she seemed pretty reluctant to help. There had to be someone else who could help.

My watch read 4:43 p.m. Andy's last practice of the day ended in 17 minutes. I checked out a couple of books, threw them in my backpack, and hopped on my bike. I was at the field in less than five minutes.

The team was going through plays. As the quarterback, Andy wore a red pinny over his jersey. It was so the rest of the team remembered they weren't supposed to tackle him because apparently football players were stupid enough to forget *not* to tackle their own quarterback.

I paced the length of the end line while I waited. My skin itched with excitement, or was that my neck prickling again.

To distract myself, I kicked around a small rock, practicing a soccer move I had learned this summer. My coach wanted me to be able to use it in my next game on Sunday. Dribble, dribble, step over, step over, and sprint with the ball. I did it over and over again; repetition was the best way to learn a new move.

The football team ended practice with a series of sprint drills. As soon as Andy was on the sideline, I dragged my bike over to him.

While he took off his shoes, I stood over him and said, "Hey."

He looked up with surprise. "Billy boy. What are you doing here?"

William, I wanted to say, but I stuck to the point.

"I was at the library looking up some more stuff about Captain Kidd." I was talking pretty fast because I was so excited. "I definitely think he buried treasure on Pirate Island. I know you were pretty sure he had, but I wasn't so sure at first. But now, I mean all the facts point to it. I still don't know exactly where he buried it, but I think we can find someone who does. We just need to look at those articles in your storage area again."

"I'm kind of over all that pirate treasure stuff." He avoided looking at me.

"Kind of over it," I repeated. I stared down at him, my head cocked to the side. "It was your idea in the first place."

A few of Andy's teammates stared at us. He looked at them and gave a little laugh. "He's a friend from school."

"His best friend. We've been best friends since we were two years old."

That was when Andy's parents had bought the house diagonally behind ours and he spoke his first word, "Friend." Now it seemed Andy had forgotten all that history between us.

"Best friends?" one of the teammates said. "Sounds more like you're the dorky side kick."

I waited for Andy to defend me, like he always did. He threw his gear in a bag and stood. Gaze on the grass, he ran his hand through his hair and shook out his stupid golden locks. "I'll meet you guys in the parking lot in a minute," he said to his teammates.

The other players walked away, laughing. I had a feeling they were laughing at me. Andy finally looked at me, but he didn't say anything.

"What do you mean you're kind of over it?" I was a

hot-air balloon of rage ready to lift off and pull Andy along with me so I could drop him over some sharp rocks.

"It's just," he said, "don't you think we're kind of old to be digging for buried treasure? We're almost in high school. Pirates are for little kids."

A dull pain throbbed in my chest, and my ears buzzed. "I didn't know searching for pirate treasure had an age limit."

He glanced over to the parking lot, bouncing on his toes. "It just doesn't seem...cool."

"So you're gonna leave me hanging?" And Kidd hanging, I thought, but didn't say. "It wasn't exactly easy to convince my sister to help us. You know we need three people to dig up the treasure. Where am I gonna find someone else?"

A horn beeped. One of his teammates hung out a car window, waving.

"Billy. I really gotta go. Warner's mom is waiting for me."

"Fine." I clenched my fists at my side, never wanting so badly to punch him. "You go have a great time with Warner and his mommy. Don't worry about your best friend or anything."

"Chill out."

"Chill out!" I shouted. It was mutiny, or desertion at the least. Where was a bucket when I needed one? My traitor best friend needed some sense knocked into him. I squeezed my fists tighter, fingernails digging into my skin. No matter how much being like Kidd had helped me out, I wasn't going to hit Andy. But I had another weapon. "Chill out! I'm not gonna chill out! Why don't you chill out? Or are you already too cool?"

He turned and walked towards the parking lot.

"Hey, Andy!" I yelled. "Maybe your mom can help me find the treasure."

He swiveled on his heels and shot fireballs at me with his eyes, his face an interesting shade of purple. "What are you talking about?"

"The letter from your mom." I forced the words out, even as I was beginning to regret turning the conversation in this direction.

He ran at me, shoved me to the ground, and jumped on top of me. He pummeled me in the stomach, each punch of painful reminder of what a terrible best friend I was. Spit soaked my face as he screamed nonsense words at me. Finally, one of his coaches pulled him off.

Arms pinned behind his back and face squinched up in agony, he yelled, "Don't talk about my mom!"

With sharp pains shooting up my stomach, I jumped on my bike and drove right across the middle of the field, leaving tire tracks behind me.

I stopped pedaling after a few blocks. My hands were shaking too much for me to ride. Since when was my best friend too cool for me? And when did I become such a jerk?

It was all smoke and mirrors. Our friendship, the person I thought I was, the treasure. Everything.

Chapter 16

Looking back on it, I want to blame my behavior on Kidd and the whole possession thing, but I know better. On the beach tonight, staring up at Andy's hulking figure, Kidd confirms that remark about Andy's mom was all Billy, not William.

Doesn't matter how awful I once acted. My ex-best friend is not welcome here.

"You might have started this treasure hunt," I tell him. "But we're—" oops, can't let him know about mine and Kidd's connection, "I'm going to finish it."

"How?" he asks. "You need three treasure hunters, right?"

"I've got them."

Just then a deep motor rumbles in the parking lot, announcing the arrival of Justin's junker. I stand and turn my back on Andy to head to the car and help unload our supplies. Andy follows behind me. Who's the magician and who's the captive audience now?

I pretend not to notice as he hovers. But once we're

unpacked, he's still hanging around and not likely to leave any time soon. It's time to enlist some help.

"Kristina, can you please tell Andy that he's not coming with us?"

Before she can answer, Andy interrupts, "You can't stop me from coming on the island."

My patience is up, and so is Kidd's. "Why would you want to come? No one wants you here. How did you even know to show up tonight?"

"I, uh..." Andy trails off, which is totally not like him. What gives?

"I invited him," Kristina says with a confidence that makes me want to smack her.

"You crossed your heart," I remind her of her promise not to tell Andy.

"I lied. You don't know how important friendship is. Your best friend should be here for this, so I made sure he was."

I'm speechless. I can't believe Kristina betrayed us— me?—but I'm itching to get on the island all the same. "Whatever!" I point a finger at Andy. "Don't even think about speaking to me."

Then I grab a few supplies and stalk off towards the tombolo. It's time Kidd has his revenge, and I'm not going to let my loser ex-best friend ruin it.

Chapter 17

After the blowout on the football field with Andy, I automatically headed towards my street, but I wasn't in the mood to go home. Once I could hold the handlebars without shaking, I pedaled in the opposite direction, not really sure where I was going. My legs (or Kidd's) knew where to take me: the beach.

The tide was pretty high, and the sandbar was covered. The island looked far away and unreachable. I imagined what it would be like to have a big pirate ship. How it would feel to sail off into the horizon, the salty wind blowing all my cares away. Was that how Captain Kidd felt when he set off on the *Adventure Galley*?

I tried not to think about what I had said to Andy. So instead I thought about what he had said to me. Did he really think pirates were for kids? Was he really giving up on hunting for Captain Kidd's treasure? Was I stupid for still wanting to find it?

At the thought of giving up the hunt, my throat constricted and I felt like I couldn't breathe. Okay, so maybe calling it quits wasn't the answer. The tightness immediately lessened, but now I felt trapped in my own body.

If I couldn't sail off into the horizon away from my cares, maybe I could swim off into it. I peeled off my shoes, socks, and t-shirt. I reached the waterline and let the waves wash over my feet. The surf was rough, well, rough for Long Island Sound. Compared to the real ocean, it was pretty pathetic.

Andy had come with my family to Martha's Vineyard earlier in the summer, and the waves there were huge. They were taller than my dad, and he's over six feet. I almost lost my bathing suit while body-surfing. Kristina didn't go in past her ankles. Andy acted like a professional surfer on his boogie board.

Forget him.

I went in up to my stomach and dove in. I swam until after sunset, watching the orange and pink sky turn dark blue as I floated on my back. My fingers and toes were pruny by the time I ventured back to the sand. A cool breeze raised goose bumps on my skin. The tide had receded to reveal some of the sandbar. I walked along it until I reached where the water lapped up both sides and danced in a swirl of dark green-blue.

In the distance, Pirate Island was a black stain against the sky. I sat down in the sand and shells and stared. I imagined Kidd's pirate ship cruising into the

Sound, its huge sails billowing in the breeze.

I pictured him and his most trusted men rowing a small boat to the island to scope out a place to hide their loot. I heard their footsteps as they trudged through the sand and into the brush, Kidd's exclamation as he found the perfect spot to hide his precious cargo, the shuffle of the shovel as it sifted through the earth.

I was more convinced than ever that Kidd had buried his treasure on Pirate Island. And that I would be the one to find it...if only I could find a little help.

"What are you doing?" asked a shrill voice from right behind me.

I jumped to my feet, fists raised, and turned to see a familiar silhouette. "Kris! What are you doing here?"

"I asked you first."

"Swimming."

She crossed her arms over her chest. "Swimming? In the sand?"

"Oh yeah. I just love the way it feels in my shorts. I was swimming in the water, you idiot."

"Well, Mom's been going nuts, wondering where you've been."

I checked my watch. I had missed dinner, and I hadn't called to say I wasn't going to be home. "Uh oh. Am I in trouble?"

She answered with a smug, "Probably."

"You're helpful."

"Well what do you expect when you don't come home for dinner? C'mon. Justin's waiting for us in his car."

"Oh, Justin," I said in a high-pitched voice. Then I pretended to throw up. "I can't believe Mom let you go out with him."

"It's all thanks to you. She let me drive around with him to look for you."

Justin helped me put my bike in his trunk, and we sped away from the beach and Pirate Island. I clamped my mouth shut for the whole ride home. I was too nervous about getting in trouble to talk. Not that anyone would've heard me because Kristina's stupid boyfriend had his band's music blasting in the car.

When we got home, my mom rushed over to give me a big hug. She rubbed my hair and then yelled at me. She was still yelling when my father got home. I had already apologized about ten times. I guess one more couldn't hurt.

"I'm sorry, Dad," I said. "I didn't feel like coming home, not after fighting with Andy."

"You and Andy had a fight," my mom said. "What was it about?"

My dad grabbed a water from the refrigerator and left the kitchen. Fights with best friends were Mom's area, not his. Not that much of anything fell into my dad's territory anymore.

"We were supposed to do this thing together," I said. "Andy decided it wasn't cool enough for him and his football friends."

My mom rubbed my hair again. "Can someone else help?"

"Kristina was already going to, but we need a third person."

"Maybe it could be a family project. What about your old mom?"

I didn't want to hurt my mom's feelings, but she wasn't exactly the third person I was looking for. Digging illegally on a possibly haunted island...yeah, definitely not Mom territory.

I slipped away to the kitchen doorway. "Thanks, but you don't have to help. It was all Andy's idea in the first place. I'm gonna try and forget about it."

"Oh, Billy." She crossed the room to give me a hug, and I almost told her to call me William. "Sometimes growing up is hard. I'm sure Andy will come around, and you'll have plenty of time to do things together."

I tried not to gag. Who needed Andy as a friend anyway? At least talking about the fight with my mom got her to take it easy on me. My punishment was that I had to do extra chores for the rest of the week instead of being grounded. My dad even promised to go to my soccer game on Saturday. He had missed most of them because of work.

As I lay in bed that night, I tried to put all thoughts of Kidd's treasure out of my mind. Without any leads—and without any friends to help me—there was really no point in looking for it anymore. Despite my efforts to forget, the image of Captain Kidd on Pirate Island stuck in my head and haunted my dreams. It was another night that I didn't get a lot of sleep.

Chapter 18

I really tried to forget about looking for Captain Kidd's treasure for the next few days. I hid all the books and materials under a stack of dirty clothes in the back of my closet. I spent hours on the computer, rereading my ghost story and making it perfect for the literary journal. I did practically a million laps in the pool. But I couldn't let the treasure hunt go (Kidd wouldn't allow it).

I went back to the library with the intention of returning the biography and borrowing books with absolutely nothing to do with pirates or islands. A novel about a boy with terminal cancer caught my attention. I found a comfortable chair by the window, but I couldn't get into the book. I stared out the glass and watched kids playing on the basketball courts.

"How goes the treasure hunt?" asked a vaguely familiar voice.

Library staffer Ken, the one who had helped me interpret Kidd's letter, peered at me with kind eyes. I shrugged. "It's not."

He pointed to the paperback about Pirate Island, the one that belonged to Andy's dad, that sat on top of my backpack. "You know my ancestors used to own not only Pirate Island but the whole town, too."

"Really?" I was surprised until I took a more critical look at Ken. Pirate Island, before it went by that name, had originally been owned by Native Americans, and I could now see a hint of his ancestors in his features.

He settled down in a nearby chair. "Back then the island was called Poquahaug. The tribe sachem—that's the chief—sold the whole thing, island and town, to European settlers for six coats, ten blankets, one kettle, twelve hatchets, twelve hoes, two dozen knives, and—"

I said it at the same time he did, "A dozen mirrors."

His eyes widened in surprise.

I picked up the paperback. "I've read it like a dozen times."

Ken nodded with approval. Then he clapped his hands together in a way that was very unlibrary-like and stood. "Well, it seems you already know all there is to know."

I sort of grunted and snorted at the same time. "Not where the treasure is."

"Sometimes finding the treasure isn't as important as looking for it. Do you understand what I'm saying?"

I answered with the truth. "Not really." Nothing was more important than finding Kidd's treasure. This I knew, though I didn't fully understand why.

He rapped his knuckle on the arm of the chair he had been sitting in. "That's okay. You will. Just keep looking, young treasure hunter." Then he disappeared down an aisle. I resumed my previous status of staring out the window.

Captain Kidd's problems filled my head and left no room for anything else.

He had been hired to be a privateer but was declared to be a pirate before he could even start the job. When he got back to New England, he turned himself into the authorities. It may have taken him a little while to do it, but he eventually did because he thought the law was on his side. What a joke!

He didn't think he had done anything wrong. He could've easily packed up his wife and daughters and taken them and his treasures far away from anyone who could prosecute him, but he tried to do the right thing. Then men he thought he could trust sent him to England to be hanged.

Not that anyone was trying to kill me or anything, but I could relate to being betrayed by someone you thought you could trust. William Kidd may have captained a ship, but he was threatened by his crew and forced to do things he didn't want to. Just like Andy always forced me to do things.

Now I had a chance to try and set things right. Give Captain Kidd's spirit a well-deserved rest. I put the tearjerker cancer book back on the shelf and tucked the books about Kidd and Pirate Island under my arm. With a determined smile, I waved to Ken on the way out of the library. I would find my way to the treasure.

Chapter 19

Friday afternoon, I locked myself in my room and lay on the bed. I stared at the ceiling for a while until I noticed something sticking into my back. I reached underneath me and found a big bouncy ball.

I threw it against the wall, and it bounced right back into my hand. I threw it again. It thumped off the wall and bounced back. Throw, thump, bounce. Throw, thump, bounce. Throw, thump, bounce. The rhythm helped me think.

"Billy!" Kris yelled from her room. "What are you doing?"

I ignored her and continued to play. Throw, thump, bounce. Throw, thump, bounce. Throw, thump, bounce. A loud knock sounded on my bedroom door.

"Billy!" Kris yelled again. "Stop banging on my wall."

I threw the ball harder. Throw, thump, bounce. She knocked on my door again and jiggled the doorknob.

"Billy!" she screamed. "Stop it, right now!"

Throw, thump, bounce. Throw, thump, bounce. Throw,

thump, bounce.

"Mom!" she shouted from outside my door.

I stopped throwing the ball long enough to hear the distinct sound of the stairs creaking under my mom's feet. Kristina whined to my mom, but I had gone back to throwing the ball and didn't hear what was said. A softer knock sounded on my door.

"Billy," my mom said. "What's going on?"

I didn't answer. I just kept bouncing the ball off the wall.

"Billy," my mom said a little louder. "Open this door now."

Throw, thump, bounce. Throw, thump, bounce. Throw, thump, bounce.

"William Ian Bonny," my mom said. "Don't make me count."

Uh oh! She had brought out the full name, and that meant business. I jumped off my bed, flipped the lock, and opened the door. My mom stood there with her arms folded across her chest. Kristina smirked at me from behind my mom's back.

"What is going on?" my mom asked.

"Nothing," I lied.

"Nothing? Then what is making all that noise?"

I held up the bouncy ball.

"Sit." My mom pointed to the bed.

I obeyed. Now was not the time to go all Captain Kidd

on her. She sat down next to me and rubbed my head like she used to when I was a little kid and couldn't fall asleep.

"I know you're still upset about your fight with Andy," she said. "But you can't go around taking it out on other things...people or walls."

She smiled and looked at me expectantly. I rewarded her with a twitch of a smile.

"Have you talked to Andy?"

I shrugged.

"Maybe you should." She continued to rub my head.

"He's never going to forgive me." Not that I wanted him to because I could never forgive him.

"Have you given him the chance?"

What would I say to him if by chance I did want him to forgive me (which I didn't)? *Sorry I read your private letter from your mom. It was Captain Kidd's fault.*

My mom accepted my silence as a "no" and patted my hand. "Why don't you give him a call tomorrow?"

"Fine." There was no way I was calling him. Mutineers don't get second chances. Andy was lucky I didn't use a bucket to knock some sense into him. Not that I wanted to kill him, but a light knock on the head might remind him who his best friend was.

"I think a big bowl of mint chocolate-chip ice cream will help cheer you up. We can put candies and chocolate syrup on top."

I shrugged. Andy's betrayal went too far for even ice

cream to heal.

"I got some orange sorbet for you, Kristina," my mom said.

I had forgotten about my sister, who stood in the open doorway. My face turned red hot when I realized she had been listening the whole time. I thought steam might pour out of my ears with the level of embarrassment I was experiencing.

Thankfully, Kris didn't mention the conversation while we ate our ice cream. My mom left the kitchen without having any and came back all dressed up, bright red lipstick on her lips. "Your father and I are going out tonight. I talked to Kris," she glanced at my sister, "and she's agreed to be nice to you...as long as you listen to her. No talking back."

I shrugged, keeping my inner-pirate in check, playing the good boy.

After my parents left, Kris looked up from her bowl, eyes wide. "If you do one thing for me tonight, I'll do whatever you want with the treasure hunt."

Whoa! That was a big offer. Meaning she could only want something big in return. Captain William (yeah, I liked the sound of that), however, would do whatever it took to get what he wanted.

"What do you need me to do?" I scraped the edges of the bowl and pretended to concentrate on getting every last drop of ice cream out of it.

Kristina tapped her spoon on the table. "Justin's band is playing a show at the teen center. And I really want to go. The only problem is it's tonight. And you can't tell Mom and Dad where I went."

"So if I let you go to Justin's show, you'll do whatever I want to help me find Captain Kidd's treasure?"

Her forehead crinkled up and she grimaced, but she squeaked out, "Yes."

"So you'll go to Pirate Island with me tomorrow." I figured I'd better grab the opportunity with both hands while I had it.

"When are you going?"

"I'll check on when it'll be low tide."

I ran to the living room, found a newspaper, and sprinted back to the kitchen. Kristina was rinsing out our ice cream bowls.

"Low tide is as 1:22 in the afternoon," I announced. "I have a soccer game in the morning, so that's perfect."

Kristina turned, hands on hips, a forced smile on her lips. "You're the boss."

"Should we put it in writing?" I wasn't taking any chances. My sister had been known to make a promise in one breath and deny it in the next.

"How about a binding handshake?" She held out her hand.

We shook on it. Score one for Captain William.

Then she did something I never expected when she

said, "You should come to the show. Maybe some of your friends will be there."

"I don't want to see Andy."

"Okay, friends other than Andy."

Funny, it took Kristina saying that for me to realize I didn't really have any other friends. I talked to my teammates at practice and games, but not any other time. Maybe it was time to branch out. Maybe Ella would be there.

"I'll go," I declared.

She looked me up and down. "Cool. But you can't wear that."

Chapter 20

My sneakers, soccer shorts, and Manchester United t-shirt seemed fine to me, but apparently they didn't pass my sister's inspection.

I rolled my eyes. "I didn't know there would be a dress code for a stupid concert at the teen center."

She poked me in the chest. "Don't start with me or I'll uninvite you."

I ran up to my room and searched around under my bed until I found an old pirate costume. The vest was a little tight, but I managed to button it up over my t-shirt. The hat still fit, as did the eye patch and hook hand. Back downstairs, I struck a pirate pose and winked at Kristina.

She took one look at me and shook her head. "No way."

"Fine. What am I supposed to wear?" Nothing in my wardrobe was anything like her tiny, sparkly top and tighter than tight jeans.

"Jeans and a button up shirt. That won't be totally embarrassing."

"Whatever!" It was too hot for jeans, but I knew Captain William couldn't win every battle with his new first mate. I threw on a pair of tan shorts and a short-sleeved polo shirt from my closet floor, clothes that no longer needed to cover up the treasure hunting materials.

A car horn honked outside, and Kristina yelled for me to come downstairs. When I got to the door, Justin was leaning against his old beat up car. Kristina embraced him, the side of her face practically attached to his chest. Gross!

He scanned my outfit. "Cool look. Messy preppy."

It didn't exactly sound like a compliment, but he nodded his head as if he approved. Not that I cared what anyone thought of my outfit.

We zoomed away from the house, Justin's screechy music blaring, and quickly arrived at the teen center. At the door, a sign read HIGH SCHOOL I.D. REQUIRED TO ENTER.

"Damn," Kristina said. "I thought it was an all-ages show."

"No worries, Tina. You're with the band." Justin escorted us to a side entrance, and no one gave us a second glance as we entered a staging area.

Kristina ushered me through a door into the main room. "You can hang out here. I'm staying backstage until the show starts."

That was where all the people were, so that was fine with me. Too bad it took me about a minute to realize I didn't know anyone there. I should have stayed home by myself. At least then I could have read. Then I remembered the paperback about Pirate Island tucked into my back pocket.

I found a table and chairs in a corner and stuck my face in the book. Kristina plopped a soda on the table before disappearing backstage.

When I was about halfway through the book, the lights dimmed. I looked up to find the chairs around me occupied. Bodies packed the area in front of the stage like pieces of candy stuffed in an airless bag. When had all these people arrived? A buzzing energy filled the air. Kristina squeezed out the door, waved when she spotted me, and pushed her way to the front of the crowd.

The lights dimmed even lower, making it impossible for me to read. Five guys sauntered onto the stage, Justin among them. The crowd screamed in excitement. I rolled my eyes. All this commotion for a stupid high-school band. Justin draped a guitar strap across his chest and poised his hands over the strings.

The drummer tapped his sticks together in time. The stage lit up, and the band screeched out a series of notes that sounded more like dying cats than music. I resisted the urge to cover my ears, knowing I might offend a fan and possibly get beat up. I clutched the book tight in my hands and channeled Kidd's spirit. He endured getting strung up on the noose twice; surely I could handle a little torture by amateur band.

An agonizing six songs and 20 minutes, 33 second later (I knew exactly how long because I watched the numbers on my digital watch tick slowly by) the torture finally stopped. I slapped my book on the table and stood up and cheered with the rest of the crowd. I mean, I clapped and yelled for a different reason than they did, but no one had to know that.

The lights came back up, and the mass of people dispersed around the room. At least half of the girls formed a line for the bathroom. I sat and reached for my book just as a girl's hand touched it. Her nails sparkled a neon pink.

"You brought a book to a concert." I looked up to see a petite blonde with shiny pink lips and a dark pink t-shirt. Boy, this girl really liked pink. It *was* really pretty on her, but it was a bit much.

I shrugged.

She said with a smile, "How very avant-garde."

Just like when Justin had called my look "messy preppy," I had no idea what "a vent guard" meant, but it seemed to be a compliment. Did all these high-school kids talk in a crazy language only they understood?

While she examined the book cover, I smiled back, sure my face was turning bright red from embarrassment. Or maybe my cheeks were warm for another reason?

"I'm Kayla. Are you a freshman?"

I was about to introduce myself, tell her my name was William and let her think I was in the incoming freshman class, not the eighth-grade one. Maybe I would say something nice about all her pinkness. But before I could do any of that, a very tall guy lurched up. Andy would have looked like a baby next to him. "You talking to my girlfriend, big guy?"

Even when I stood, my head only reached his armpits. His beefy biceps pulsed under a way too small t-shirt. He took a menacing step closer, and I got a whiff of stinky armpits. I backed up until my butt hit the table. The guy snatched the book from Kayla.

"Leave him alone, Aiden," she said. "I was just saying hi."

"Who brings a book to a concert?" Aiden looked over my head, like he was addressing the crowd and not me. He slapped the book against my chest. "Stay away from my girlfriend."

I sensed old Billy creeping back from deep inside and swallowed a few times to keep him down. My nostrils flared as I inhaled a deep breath, summoning my pirate strength. Mutiny would not be tolerated.

Before I really knew what I was doing, my hand cocked back and swung forward, right into Aiden's chin. Good thing I didn't have a bucket, or I might've really hurt him.

He staggered back slightly, his eyes widening in shock. Was he surprised I had hit him or that it actually hurt? Either way, my veins were pumping pure pirate adrenaline. My chair flew across the floor...from *me* throwing it!

A bystander yelled, "Fight!"

The crowd formed a circle around the three of us. Kayla grabbed Aiden's arm to restrain him. He rubbed his chin where I had hit him and lunged. A body blocked his path. Hands encircled my upper arms, sharp nails pierced my skin, and I was pulled backward.

Kristina had to yell in my ear to be heard over all the shouting, "We need to get out of here!"

"My book!" I cried.

I barely heard her groan in all the noise erupting from the masses around us. Aiden and the person who had jumped in between us were scuffling on the ground. Justin's orange hair emerged from the tangle of body parts on the floor. Whoa, Justin had saved me from getting pummeled.

Spotting my book on the floor, I grabbed it and followed Kris backstage. We were the only people there; everyone else was out front in the middle of the action.

She shoved me into a corner behind a loosely hung curtain. "Don't move. I've gotta help Justin."

My breath came in raspy bursts. My hand stung, and I rubbed it gingerly. Nothing felt broken. I wondered how Aiden's face felt. My pirate adrenaline began to work its way out of my veins. Then I began to worry.

I had punched a high-school guy in the face. What kind of trouble was I going to be in? Would they call the police? Would I be arrested?

I hunched down in my dark corner, the Pirate Island book under my armpit, and worried the minutes away. When my hand had clocked Aiden in the face, it hadn't felt like mine. Not in an out-of-control kind of feeling, more of an in-someone-else's-control kind of way. I should have recognized the signs of what I was becoming—of what Kidd was doing to me—but my whole head was full of smoke and mirrors. What I could see was distorted and confusing and didn't make any sense. (Kidd is a far better magician than Andy ever could be.)

Chapter 21

Nervously nibbling on my nail, I decided I would take whatever punishment they gave me like a pirate. Kidd had faced his death when it came; I would do the same. Though I remained hidden behind the curtain.

The door banged open, and I held my breath. A wave of shouting and clattering washed over to my hiding place and quieted when the door clapped shut. The curtain fluttered open. I closed my eyes against the light, dim as it was, hoping it wasn't a cruel fate that awaited me. My neck prickled with the imaginary noose.

"It's chaos out there," said Kristina. It was safe to open my eyes. Kristina's and Justin's silhouettes were framed by the curtain. "I don't think anyone knows exactly what happened, and we're leaving before they figure it out."

She grabbed me by the arms and man-handled me out the back exit into the empty alley, Justin following along. I kept my head down and my gaze on my feet as we walked back to the car. Luckily we didn't encounter anyone. They must have all stayed inside the teen center.

Once I was safely buckled into the backseat, we cruised down the street with the windows closed. No mind-numbing music blared through the speakers. No air entered the stifling car. The thump of the ancient engine was the only sound in the car. My stomach twisted. I sniffled in the humid air, trying not to gag. I couldn't quite believe I'd actually punched Aiden. (Probably because it was really Kidd who punched him, but I suppose that was a technicality at this point.)

Kristina pounded the floor with her feet and glared at me. "What were you thinking?"

"I—ah," I croaked out. William would have said something smart, but right then I was scared back into being Billy, and I had no good answer. "I guess I was thinking of Captain Kidd and what he would have done if someone had threatened him."

She shook her head, narrowing her eyes. "I can't believe you. Picking a fight with a varsity member of the football team."

A football player! Like Andy. My guilt washed away like sand eroding in a hurricane. The guy deserved everything he got. I hoped Justin had given Aiden a black eye. "Captain Kidd killed a mutineer with a bucket. I only punched a guy." William was back.

"Billy!" Kristina leaned farther into the back. "This isn't the sixteenth century. You can't go around acting like a pirate."

"Seventeenth century," I corrected her, earning myself a death glare.

Justin surprised us both by chuckling. Kristina turned her glare on him.

"I don't know. That was pretty awesome." He lisped over the words a little. I stuck my head between the two front seats and noticed a bloody slit in his lower lip.

"Sorry about your lip," I mumbled. Great, now I owed him one.

Justin parked the car in front of my house. "Don't worry about it. That fight will be legend. Totally made me look like a bad—"

"Justin!" Kristina said. "Enough. I don't need you encouraging him." She tossed the house keys to me. "Go inside and get ready for bed. I'll be in in a few."

I was in bed, teeth brushed and everything, by the time footsteps came up the stairway. I touched the cold cover of the Pirate Island paperback, which I had tucked under my pillow. Kristina knocked and opened my door a crack. The hallway light created a sliver on the floor like a tiny moon. I scooted to a sitting position and stared at the beige carpet as she settled on the edge of my bed.

Good-boy Billy emerged. "Please don't tell Mom about what happened tonight."

"Of course I won't tell Mom," she said. "She'd kill both of us.... I can't believe you did that."

"Are you mad?" My cheeks warmed in

embarrassment. I didn't want my sister to know how much I didn't want her to be mad at me. And how much I missed hanging out with her.

She ruffled my hair and grinned, her teeth gleaming in the light from the hallway. "Nah. That guy Aiden is a jerk. He deserved to get punched in the face."

"Why does a pretty girl like Kayla go out with him?" A few days ago, I would've asked the same thing about Kristina and Justin, but after tonight, I had to give the guy some credit. He really saved my pirate butt.

"Is my little brother interested in an older girl?" Her smile grew wider.

My face heated to erupting volcano level. "No, I don't —"

"Don't worry. I get it. All that pink can be cute to some guys."

"I don't like her," I nearly shouted. "I like Ella, a girl in my grade." Oops, hadn't meant to admit that.

Kristina laughed. "Okay, you don't like Kayla." She shifted on the bed. "You still want to go to Pirate Island tomorrow?"

"Yeah. Low tide is at 1:22," I reminded her.

"So you really think that Captain Kidd buried his treasure there."

"Yes." I refrained from spouting out all the evidence in support of it. Kristina was holding up her end of the deal, but I was sure she didn't care about the specifics.

"Okay," she said. "I'll see if Mom can give us a ride to the beach."

"Really?" I asked. "Not Justin."

She shrugged. "Nope. He's working." That explained why she didn't mind hanging out with me. Oh well. At least she was going. "Goodnight, Billy."

I said goodnight and right before she closed the door, yelled, "Hey!" Kristina turned back to me, a silhouette so I couldn't make out her features, which I was glad of. "Do you think you could start calling me William instead of Billy?"

"Feeling all grown up after tonight?"

"Something like that," I mumbled, though I was thinking more about William Kidd than Billy Bonny.

"Sure...William." I heard her giggle softly before shutting my door.

As I lay in bed, my hand throbbed from the punch, which I kept picturing over and over again in my mind. I still couldn't believe I'd really punched a varsity football player. I wished Andy had been there to see it. I could tell him, but he probably wouldn't believe me, and we weren't talking anyway.

Captain Kidd's ghost stayed out of my dreams that night. He had been in my head all day long, so I guess he didn't see the point of interrupting my sleep.

Chapter 22

After a quick breakfast the next morning, my mom rushed Kristina and me into the car to head to my game. Both true to our word, neither of us said a single thing about the night before. My mom's trouble radar must have been on the fritz because she didn't notice anything was up.

I tried not to think about Pirate Island during warm-ups. It was easier to forget it once the game started; the intense play required all my attention. My dad was there as promised, though he had to leave early for work.

The other team scored first, but we pulled out the win with two goals in the second half. My coach was happy with me because I tried the new step-over move. The step-over part had worked great, though I happened to kick the ball a little too far and couldn't sprint fast enough to catch up with it. Coach said to keep practicing and I'd get it perfect in the next game.

I was hyped up from the win as we drove to the beach. My stomach somersaulted as I remembered why we were going there. I took a deep breath, hoping William would reemerge when I needed him.

Kristina told my mom we'd walk back home. That way we'd have plenty of time to explore Pirate Island. It was 1:07 p.m., and the sandbar was almost at its widest.

I was wearing my uniform but had switched my shin guards and cleats for socks and sneakers. Even though it was a warm day, it was overcast, so there was hardly anyone else on the beach, just lots of seagulls. Shells crunched under our shoes as we walked down the sandbar.

"What do you think we should look for?" I asked.

"I don't know," Kristina said. "Whatever we want. Does it really matter?"

"Of course it matters. How are we supposed to find Captain Kidd's treasure if we don't have a plan?"

"You still think you're going to find pirate treasure on the island?"

"Maybe. Why else would we be here?" Was she going to pull an Andy on me and tell me pirates were for babies?

"I don't know. I thought since you and Andy have been fighting, you kind of needed another friend to hang out with. I know I'm just your sister, but we have fun hanging out."

I tried not to pout over the fact that Kristina was here out of pity. I would have preferred to think she had come because of the deal we made. We walked the rest of the way in silence, the wind whistling off the water on either side of us.

Lately, I *had* missed hanging out with my sister, which was stupid. Or maybe it wasn't. Kidd had loved his family. His desire to keep them from facing a life on the run was the main reason he hadn't fled to the Caribbean when he realized he might be in trouble with the law for his alleged piracy. So I figured it was okay to like spending time with my family.

Soon we made it to the end of the tombolo. On the island, we faced the problem of the makeshift fence that was supposed to keep people from bothering the nesting birds. Kristina and I followed the sand around to the west side of the island, the opposite way Andy and I had traveled the night the Coast Guard showed up. I stopped walking when we came across a section of the fence that had been pulled down.

I stood and stared at the opening.

"Well, are we going in?" Kristina finally asked.

"You want to go into the trees?"

"Sure. Why not?"

"I've never gone onto that part of the island. I've only ever walked around it."

"Don't be such a scaredy-cat."

"I'm not scared." Pirates don't get scared. "It's just that we might disturb the birds."

"Nesting season is almost over. There's nothing to worry about."

Nesting season would end in a couple of weeks. I

knew that from my research. There were probably some birds on the island, but all of their eggs would've hatched by now. I had made sure that if we did dig for treasure, we wouldn't be disturbing them. Still, it was pretty dark behind the fence. On the other hand, it wasn't very pirate-like of me to chicken out.

"Fine," I said. "Let's go."

Maybe I should have gone in first, but I let Kristina take the lead. I followed her around a boulder and through the break in the fence. The trees weren't really all that thick towards the middle. Wild brush and vines snaked all along the ground, but a few paths wound through the undergrowth. The wind and waves were a distant hum from the middle of the island.

"Let's check out the old monastery ruins," she said.

"How do you know about those?" I had read about them in the Pirate Island paperback but hadn't expected her to know of them.

"Oh, who doesn't know that?"

"Well, I didn't before I read about them. Have you been here before?"

"Maybe. Justin likes it out here. He says the quiet allows him to hear the music he's working on in his head."

"Does the quiet let him hear the voices in his head, too?"

Kristina punched me hard in the stomach. I fell onto my knees.

"Why do you have to make fun of Justin all the time?" she asked.

I tilted my head to look up at her. "Why do you like him so much?"

She smiled, a faraway look in her eyes. "I don't know. He's cool. I like to hear him play his music. He writes songs for me. And he came to the rescue of my puny brother who picked a fight with a football player." I smiled when I thought of my pirate moment. (As scary as it had been, it also had given me a weird sense of courage.) "Why don't you like him?"

"I don't know. He looks like a punk to me. And he calls you Tina."

She offered a hand to help me up. "You know, you don't have to hate him just because he's my boyfriend. Justin's really nice. Maybe you'd like him if you gave him a chance."

"Maybe." *Maybe not* was more like it. I'd probably never like a guy who called my sister Tina and sported bright orange hair. The conversation was getting too mushy for me. "Where are these ruins?"

Kristina headed south. We hadn't walked more than five minutes when we came across an old doorway—minus the door and whatever it was supposed to lead to. It was made of large stones, layered like bricks. The doorway rounded out as it went up, but the two sides met in a point at the very top. There was about two feet of stones on either side of it and above it. On one side, though, the stone went up another couple of feet—in what kind of looked like a chimney, only it wasn't hollow. I guess the structure had deteriorated in a lopsided way.

"I dare you to go and stand under it," Kristina said in a hushed tone.

"I don't know," I said in my library voice.

What if Pirate Island was haunted? And the skies opened up when I stepped under the doorway? And the earth shook? And stones fell on my head?

"I'll do it," she said.

Before I could stop her, or even say anything, she was standing under the stones, framed by the doorway. The sky didn't open up, but I thought she was crazy brave.

Captain William abandoned me, and I glanced around nervously, waiting for the earthquake. "Kris, get out of there. What if those things fall on your head?"

"Oh, stop worrying."

She said it as if I really had nothing to worry about, although her voice remained quieter than normal. She rested her elbow on the edge of the archway, stuck out her hip, and smiled stupidly, as if posing for her prom picture.

"Seriously, Kris," I said, my voice a little louder. "The island is haunted. I don't think the ghosts of Captain Kidd or the Native Americans who sold the island would be very happy with you for fooling around."

"What could possibly happen? It's daylight."

The words were barely out of her mouth when a loud screech filled the air. It sounded like it was coming from right behind her, but I couldn't see past her and the archway.

"What is that?" she said in a whisper.

I was mute, my mouth glued shut. I stared at her, sure my eyes were as big as her saucer ones, as another screech echoed through the trees. My knees shook in fear. Captain Kidd, I thought, is that you?

Chapter 23

A third screech cut through my bones. This was it, I was sure Kidd's ghost was coming for us. Andy's adventures would finally be the death of me. Too bad he wasn't here to suffer the same fate.

"Billy?" Kristina asked. "What is that?"

"I think it's behind you." My whisper was hoarse, barely audible.

I was frozen, all except for my left eyelid, which began to twitch and then wouldn't stop. A full minute passed while we stared at each other. Another ear-splitting cry pierced the air.

Kristina's gaze darted around and landed on the ground. She grabbed a loose stick, raised it above her head, and turned. She remained in the doorway, blocking my view of what had been behind her. I hardly breathed for fear of making a noise.

"There's nothing here." She turned back to face me.

My arms and shoulders thawed first, and then my legs. Though my eye continued twitching. I squeezed into the archway with her and peered out the other side. There were only the same trees and brush as on the rest of the island. We looked at each other again, confused. Kristina grabbed another stick and handed it to me.

"Ready?" she whispered.

I nodded, trying not to show how scared I was. Kristina crept out of the archway. I followed her towards a large tree with a dark, gnarled trunk. A branch cracked under my sneaker. The loudest screech yet sent me shaking back under the archway. Kris gestured with her finger for me to come closer.

"I think it's behind that tree," she whispered. She pointed in the direction she wanted me to go around the tree. Then she indicated she would go the other way. On her fingers, she counted off to three and said, "Go!"

As I darted around the tree, I was prepared for the worst: pirate ghost, monster, giant man-eating rat. Instead I found...a bird. A stupid, gangly bird stuck in a wooden cage.

I caught Kristina's shocked gaze, and we instantly broke out laughing hysterically. I laughed so hard I had to lean against the tree to stay on my feet. My stomach hurt, and tears streamed from my eyes. She was bent over at the waist, gasping for breath.

When my eyes finally cleared, I studied the bird, which I decided on further inspection was really quite pretty. It was about two feet tall with snow-white feathers and a black beak. Its sticklike legs were also black, but they ended in yellow feet. The feathers on the back of its neck and head were all puffed up.

"What is it?" asked Kristina.

"A snowy egret."

It was one of the birds that commonly nested on the island. I realized it wasn't stuck in a cage but a lobster pot. Wire snaked all around the pot.

"Why's it in there?" Kristina asked.

I shrugged; like I would know why some bird was stuck in a lobster pot.

"Should we let it out?" she asked.

"I don't know," I said. "It looks pretty angry."

She rolled her eyes. "Scaredy-cat."

The bird had quieted down, and the feathers on the back of its head began to flatten. We had probably scared it half to death. Kristina stared at it thoughtfully. Feeling antsy, I shook the stiffness out of my legs by wiggling my knees back and forth. We should have been looking for clues to find Kidd's loot, not wasting time with a bird.

"Can we get moving?" I asked. Now that the fear had worn off, a gnawing impatience plagued me. (More like Kidd's gnawing impatience, but at the time—and even sometimes now—I couldn't recognize if it was his emotion or mine.)

"No." She held a finger to her lips, like she was thinking hard.

"But we came here to look for treasure. Not stare at a stupid bird."

"Give me a minute to think."

My pirate temper rose. "You've already had plenty of time to think. You've been staring at that bird forever."

"Shut up and let me think!"

"Fine."

It was no use arguing with Kristina when she was determined. I sat on the ground and leaned against the tree. The egret craned its neck to look at me. Its eyes were bright yellow with black in the center. It stared at me as if I was the reason it was in the pot. I stuck out my tongue. The bird snapped its bill and squawked.

"Kris," I said. "C'mon."

"I think we should let it out," she said.

"Bad idea. What if it attacks us?"

The feathers on the back of the egret's head lay flat now, but I imagined it was still pretty scared, and angry.

"It's just a bird," she said. "What could it possibly do?"

Hadn't she ever watched those animals attack shows? Birds were descendants of the dinosaurs; they could be pretty vicious. "Oh, I don't know. Maybe peck out our eyes or scratch us to death. It's a wild animal. It could do anything."

"We can't leave it there to die."

I let out a slow breath of frustration. She was right. We couldn't leave an innocent bird—an endangered bird—

trapped.

"Fine," I said. "Let's do it."

Chapter 24

My lukewarm attitude over freeing the bird quickly turned to ice-cold fear as the bird channeled its inner dinosaur. Instead of squawking, it made a kind of roaring noise and flapped its wings in a frantic blur of white.

In a crouch, Kristina crept towards the pot, dodging closer and then farther away as the egret pecked at her through the slats. As she moved in one last time, the bird went for her head. She screamed and ran away, flapping her arms as she bolted, looking very much like a bird.

I nearly laughed, but the glare she zoomed in my direction made me suck the chuckle back in with a hiccup noise. Then I ended up actually getting the hiccups.

Not feeling particularly brave myself, I walked around the far side of the pot, looking for an opening large enough for an egret to fit through, but I didn't see any. The pot had no bottom, and it didn't look like the bird was tangled with the wire, which was a good sign. If we could get the pot over the egret's head, it would probably be able to fly away without us having to touch it. I hoped we could do it without losing a finger, or an eye.

I picked up the stick I had used earlier and tried to pry up the edge of the pot. It tipped, but as it moved, the egret squawked and flailed and almost got caught in the wire.

I rubbed my temples, trying to massage a good idea into my brain, and thought about what Captain Kidd would do. He wouldn't let a stupid bird stand in the way of pirate treasure, that was for sure. But would he leave the bird there to suffer, an endangered bird at that?

With the stick poking into my palm as I leaned on it, my conscious and my inner pirate duked it out over whether to help the bird or ditch it.

While I struggled to organize my thoughts, Kristina picked up three sturdy sticks. She handed one to me. "We can use them to lift the pot straight up and over the bird."

I tried to ignore the voice of Kidd yelling in my head, "Forget the bird! Focus on the treasure!"

Under Kristina's direction, we tried lifting the pot by slipping the sticks through the top slot, but our arms weren't long enough to reach the opposite end.

We tried shimmying each of our sticks under the pot in the corners. It slowly began to rise and wobbled as it went higher. Once we got it a foot off the ground, it tipped towards me. The egret screeched in panic. We dropped the pot back down, but the bird only screeched louder.

It would have made for a good show if *I* hadn't been

the star of it: *Escapades of Captain William and Friends, Episode Outtakes.*

I crouched, stuck my face as close to the pot as I could without getting it pecked off, and screeched right back. The egret shut up in an instant.

Kristina laughed. "Nice job. Let's try it like this."

We tried another complicated setup with the sticks at diagonals, only to fail again. Kristina threw her sticks down in disgust. The bird was now squawking its head off.

"Yell at it again," she moaned as she rubbed her forehead.

"Really?"

"Just make it shut up so I can think a minute."

I screamed, imagining how stupid Andy would have thought I looked. Then I remembered Andy and I were no longer friends and I didn't care what he would think, so I shrieked even louder. The bird opened its beak and roared at me. I roared back. It bobbed its head as if to say, "Who do you think you are?" But it also quieted down.

Kristina snapped her fingers with a determined air. She looked at me with a pitying expression. "It's the only way."

Uh oh! What exactly was she thinking?

"We lift the pot with our hands," she said, "and then hit the ground. Make sure to cover your head. You know, just in case."

Yup, she'd lost it. "Are you nuts?"

"Hopefully it will fly away."

I threw my hands up. "Fine. Whatever. Let's get this over with." Anything to get back to treasure hunting.

"Ready?" Kris bent at the knees. "And lift."

We threw the pot off the bird. I dropped on my stomach, with my face in the dirt and my hands covering the back of my head but an eye peeking out the side. Every step the bird took with those tiny webbed feet felt like an earthquake. Air rushed across my neck as it flapped its wings. It screeched, and I swear it looked me right in the eye. Another blast of air assaulted me, and then the bird took off, its cries fading into the distance.

I dared to look up and saw the egret's majestic white wings against the gray sky. It wasn't until its form disappear beyond the canopy of trees that I felt like I could breathe again. Then my chest swelled with a different sensation, one of pride.

Kristina and I leaped up and cheered in triumph. We danced and skipped around. Then a horrifying thought occurred to me, squelching my joy like a bucket of cold water to the face. "What time is it?"

"I don't know. Why?"

"The tide!"

She inhaled sharply and slapped a hand over her mouth. She didn't have to say a thing. We ran back through the break in the fence and to the tombolo. It was still pretty wide at our end and at the far end by the beach. In the middle, though, water lapped up on both sides, covering it completely. My heart sank right to the bottom of my feet and buried itself in the sand.

Chapter 25

Every second we stared at the tombolo, it disappeared farther underneath the incoming tide.

"We can still make it," Kristina said. "Right?"

"Maybe." My voice cracked with the lie.

"Well there's no time to think about it." She walked onto the tombolo without looking back. I hurried after her. When we reached the water, she stopped.

"What's the matter?"

"I'm not ruining my new sandals." She flipped them off her feet and grabbed them before stepping into the water. "It's warm."

I stood at the edge of where the sand disappeared under the water, and hesitated, fumbling for any excuse not to have to stick my feet in there. "You're gonna get all cut up. You know the sandbar's full of broken shells, and glass from busted bottles collects up here."

"I don't care," she said over the rushing wind that always seemed to blow out there like we were in the middle of an ocean. "I paid for these sandals with my own money.

Besides, I walked around barefoot all summer and the bottom of my feet are pretty tough."

No pirate worth his gold would let his sister be brave when he was being a coward. "Fine. But don't come crying to me when a big piece of glass slices your foot."

I left my shoes on. They could get wet, as long as my feet were safe. I had my soccer team to think about. I sloshed through the water, which was getting higher every minute.

We were only ten feet or so past where the water had overtaken the tombolo, and it was already up to my knees. The farther out we went, the slicker the shells and sand became.

I was careful to test the footing of each step before putting all my weight down. My sneakers grew very waterlogged, and heavy. The current dragged at my planted foot. The crosscurrent tugged my other foot down as I tried to lift it.

It happened in slow motion. My planted foot started to slide. Then both feet were sucked all the way down. I was face up in Long Island Sound. I struggled to keep my head above the water as the current pulled me under. Saltwater rushed into my nose and mouth. The water couldn't have been more than a few feet deep, but it didn't matter. I once learned that it only takes two inches of water to drown a person. Staring up through the water, the sky took on a distorted look. The sun broke through the clouds at that moment, heaven opening up to welcome me.

No, not me. Us. Me and Kidd.

The realization hit me harder than a gale-force wind. It would've knocked the breath out of me if my lungs weren't already filling with water. One way for Kidd's spirit to leave this world was through me...the death of me!

Billy, William—whoever I was now—screamed to fight, but my limbs were too heavy to move.

I was paralyzed. I was drowning.

Chapter 26

A hand grabbed me and pulled me back into the world of the living. I coughed up water. I wheezed until I could suck in a fresh breath. Kristina's brown eyes stared down at me, wider than I'd ever seen them. Her hand held tight to my jersey.

"We've gotta go back!" she yelled. "We're not even halfway yet and the water's getting too deep."

The wind blew in strong gusts, whipping her words away. The sun disappeared back behind the clouds. Kristina's hair snapped across her face. She wiped it away with the hand that held her sandals.

"C'mon!" she shouted.

My breath had returned in shallow puffs, but I couldn't talk. Kristina finally let go of my shirt to grab onto my arm. She guided me back towards Pirate Island, navigating through the water so fast that I didn't have time to check my footing. I stumbled along behind her.

Back on the island, I sat on the sand and rested my back against a warm rock. Kristina hovered over me.

"It's fine," I managed to say in a hoarse voice. "I'm fine."

She ruffled my hair, and little specks of water shot everywhere. She giggled. I pulled off my shoes, dumped the water out of them, and laid them out on the rock next to her perfectly dry sandals.

"Nice job," I said. "Keeping your shoes dry."

"Oh, yeah," she said. "I guess I only needed one hand to pull you out of the water."

She had really come through for me. As embarrassing as it was going to be, I had to thank her.

I opened my mouth, but she waved her hand and said, as if reading my mind, "Don't thank me. It was my fault. It was stupid to think we could make it back. I know better than to try to beat the tide. The current's too strong, the way it pulls at you from both sides. I'm sorry, Billy...sorry, William."

Hearing my sister call me the name I shared with Kidd—the name I told her to call me—sent a shiver through me. I was William now, whether I wanted to be or not.

Instead of focusing on the life-and-death struggle with Kidd under the water, I concentrated on the rough sand beneath my fingers, the wind in my hair, and the worried look on Kristina's face. I pulled off my soaked socks and flung them at her. She screamed and ducked, and the socks landed in the sand. I retrieved them and put them on the rock next to my shoes.

"What now?" She sat next to me, leaning against the rock.

"I guess we wait," I said. "They'll be another low tide in twelve hours or so."

"That's a long time. Mom'll be worried."

"I don't know what else we can do. Maybe you can call Mom on your cell. Tell her we're having dinner at your friend's house or something."

I had asked my mom to get me a cell phone, but she said I was too young. All of my friends had them, but she said I didn't need one until high school. I'm glad she didn't say, "If all your friends jumped off a bridge, would you do that, too?" I hate when she says stuff like that. Getting a cell phone is nothing like jumping off a bridge after your stupid friends, something Andy would totally do.

Besides I was more likely to jump off a bridge because of a certain pirate, not because of my non-existent friends.

"I've got a better idea." Kristina pulled her phone out of her pocket and squinted at the screen. "Stupid phone. I don't have any service."

"Who are you calling?"

Instead of answering, she got up and walked away, holding up her phone. I guessed she was trying to find service. I followed her. About 20 feet from where we left our shoes, she stopped and tapped the screen. She held it up to one ear and plugged the other with her finger.

"Justin?" she said loudly. "It's Tina."

I grumbled at the nickname.

"Tina!" she shouted at the phone. "Listen, William and I are stuck on Pirate Island."

She pulled the phone away from her ear and looked at it. Then she walked another few feet towards the water. "Justin? Hello? Are you there?" She waited for an answer. "Yeah. We're stuck on Pirate Island. Can you borrow a sailboat and come get us?"

Kristina had to repeat the question four times before Justin got the whole thing. Either he was being really stupid or her service was really bad. I was banking on him being stupid.

"Great," she said into the phone. "What side is the east side?"

We were practically on the east side of the island. I poked her arm and pointed at a rock not far from us. "That's the east side."

"Never mind!" she shouted. "William knows...I said William knows. Okay. See you in a little while. Bye." She clicked off and put the phone back in her pocket. "Justin is coming to get us."

"I figured," I said. "Captain Charming to the rescue."

She slapped me on the arm. "Don't be so sarcastic. He's doing us a favor."

"Fine. Where's he gonna get a boat from?"

"He's a busboy at the yacht club."

"Oh. A rock star and a busboy. What a dreamy combination."

Kristina pushed me onto the sand. My shirt and shorts were still pretty wet, so the tiny granules stuck to them. I got up and tried to brush it off, but it stuck to my hands instead. "Thanks a lot."

"I thought you were gonna lay off Justin."

I *had* said I was going to give Lover Boy a chance, due to him keeping me from getting my face mashed in by that Neanderthal football player Aiden. But just because I was giving him a chance didn't mean I had to *think* nice things about him. I would try to be better about not making fun of him out loud.

Keeping far away from the sandbar, I washed my hands in the water calmly lapping up on the beach. "You were saying Justin is a busboy at the yacht club."

"Right," she said. "One of the yacht club members works for ESPN, and the guy offered Justin free sailing lessons in exchange for helping him do some work on his house. He said Justin could use the boat anytime."

"Wait. Was this guy named Charlie Stewart?" Andy and I watched his show all the time...well, we used to.

"Yeah. How did you know?"

"He's only like the most famous ESPN announcer there is, and he has his own show. He lives in town. I can't believe Justin actually knows Charlie Stewart. I saw him in a restaurant one time and almost asked him for an autograph."

Kristina rolled her eyes. "How brave of you."

"I'm plenty brave." When I was acting like a pirate anyway, not so much when I was drowning. Or maybe I was acting like a pirate when I was drowning. It was getting harder and harder to figure out what was what.

"I'm going to wait over there for Justin." Kristina pointed to the rock on the east side of the island. "That's where he's gonna meet us, right?"

I nodded, and she walked away. I went to pick up our shoes. Kristina silently stared at the water. I watched her pick up sand and let it run through her fingers. I think she was mad at me for making fun of Lover Boy. I would have to try and be nice to him when he picked us up. That would be easy enough, especially if I was going to get to do it while riding in Charlie Stewart's boat.

It wasn't long before a small sailboat approached the island. Captain Charming was there to rescue us. Only, this captain wore black clothes and had bright blue hair. He wasn't exactly making it easy for me to like him.

Chapter 27

Given that I was riding on a boat—I still couldn't believe it was Charlie Stewart's boat—I thought there was a good chance Kidd might highjack my mind, so I kept my mouth shut to prevent anything nasty about Justin from slipping out.

It was tight quarters on the boat. I had expected something bigger, but I should have anticipated it being small if Justin could man it singlehandedly. With amazingly steady sea legs, I stood on deck as we sailed away from Pirate Island.

Out on the open water, the waves sang a song as they splashed against the hull. I inhaled the salty air, droplets of water hitting my face. The fear of nearly drowning ebbed away. I felt home.

(Rather Kidd did, but at that point, it was the same thing.)

I imagined him at the helm of the *St. Antonio*, his privateering sloop, gliding through Long Island Sound and dropping anchor at Pirate Island to bury his fortune there.

The scene played out like a memory.

I wore a velvety black hat with a feather sticking out of it, like I'd seen Kidd wear in pictures. The sails were more yellow than white, and the hull had lost its shiny luster long ago. The boat listed slightly to the left and creaked and moaned, showing its age. The crew dropped anchor, and I set off on the dinghy, keeping my balance as it ran aground. A full moon lit my path to the center of the island.

This is a good spot to bury treasure.

I longed for my pirate costume until I realized that it might be insulting to Kidd to dress up in cheap outfit and pretend to be a pirate. The lurch of Charlie Stewart's boat brought me back to the present. The boat lurched again, and I bumped into Kristina, who shouted, "Watch out!"

With his back to us, Justin waved his hand and yelled, "Sorry! I'm still new at this!"

It seemed we were in a permanent tilt to the starboard side and heading away from shore rather than towards it. Kristina grabbed hold of the railing and turned a scowl on me as if it were my fault and not Lover Boy's. I crossed the few steps it took to reach Justin and asked if I could help.

"Yeah." He pointed to his right. "Grab that rope and pull as hard as you can."

I did, and the boat tipped back to a safer position.

He offered an out of breath, "Thanks," as he continued

to adjust the sails. Finally, the boat was back on track towards the harbor. Looking rather green, Kristina slumped down right on the deck floor.

"It's much easier when I'm out here with Charlie," a red-faced Justin admitted.

That opened up a safe topic to talk about. "That's really cool that you know Charlie Stewart." Now Kristina couldn't accuse me of not putting in an effort.

"Oh, yeah." Justin shrugged and kept his eyes on the sails. "He's pretty famous, I guess."

My mouth hung open over his offhanded response. "He's only the greatest sports announcer ever."

"I don't really watch that many sports."

"Not even the highlights?"

"Nah."

"Oh." The wind picked up the word and sent it out to sea.

Lover Boy remained distracted with trimming the sails, so I happily fell back into silence and enjoyed the rock and tilt of the ride.

When we got to the harbor, I helped Justin tie up the boat, without any mishaps. Despite his earlier troubles, I was almost impressed by his sailing knowledge. If only he didn't have blue hair, and if only he wasn't dating my sister.

My legs wobbled more on dry land than they had on the boat. I was happy to relax in the backseat of Justin's junker as he gave us a ride home. The circumstances of my near-drowning experience replayed in my head. Had Kidd's spirit somehow imbedded itself in me? Had he really wanted me to die? (I was finally starting to admit to myself that my interest in Kidd was no longer one-sided, and that somehow, the Captain's spirit had begun to influence me.)

I was exhausted by the time we got home. I made it to the kitchen before collapsing into a chair, my face down on the table. Kristina was outside, saying good-bye to Justin. She banged into the house, and two sets of creaky footsteps headed upstairs, letting me know she hadn't been able to part with Lover Boy after all. Ugh! I was too tired to care.

When I finally picked up my head, I saw there were three notes on the kitchen table, all written in my mom's neat handwriting. The first one said that my mom and dad had a dinner appointment with clients and they would be home around 9:00. How boring to be doing work on a Saturday night? At least they had left us money to order food.

I didn't think much about that note because the second one made my stomach do a somersault in my abdomen. It was from Andy. He had called. After what I'd said to him about his mom, I could hardly believe it was true.

I should call him, good-boy Billy thought.

No way, argued Captain William. He's a jerk. He doesn't deserve you as a friend. He burned the friendship that day on the football field. And you were right to talk about his mom.

I frowned. Was I really arguing with myself? Or was I arguing with Kidd? Did it matter? Either way, I was acting crazy.

The suffocating sensation of drowning filled my chest, and my heart thudded fast, fast, faster.

The word "friend" had such meaning between us, the first word Andy spoke...and he had said it about me. A friendship like ours was too good to let go. I grabbed the kitchen phone and ran up to my room.

When Andy answered, I didn't give him a chance to say anything. "Look. I'm sorry about what I said. That note was between you and your mom. I should've kept my big mouth shut."

Silence greeted me on the other end. Finally, he said in a measured voice, "Yeah, you should've." More silence.

I deserve this, I told myself.

Andy spoke again, "But it was pretty gutsy of you, especially after I made fun of you for wanting to look for Captain Kidd's treasure. I mean, I was the one who started you on the whole thing."

"Uh..." Did he really admit that?

"Did you want to keep looking? Maybe we'll get rich. Or maybe we'll get the pants scared off of us by Kidd's ghost. Either way, I'm in."

I pictured us lurching away from Pirate Island with our pants down at our ankles. The image was more funny than scary. I cracked up, and so did Andy. My grin stretched all the way across my face; I had my best friend back. When I invited him for dinner, he said he'd be right over.

I felt like myself again, and was happy...for the moment.

Chapter 28

I went in search of Kristina and found her and Justin sitting very close to each other on the living room couch. She had a menu in her hands, but she wasn't looking at it. Their faces were very close together, and I had a feeling they had been doing something I absolutely did not want to witness. In fact, I suspected it was something I would go out of my way to avoid seeing. Now that I wasn't dead-tired, Justin being there was really starting to annoy me. My mom definitely would not have approved. With my parents gone, didn't that make it my job to stop this?

I cleared my throat so loudly it sounded like a monster coughing. "I thought Justin was going home."

They both jumped, apparently too involved in their love-fest to notice me. Kristina quickly stood up, grabbed my arm, and dragged me into the kitchen.

"Justin's having dinner with us," she said in a quiet voice.

"What makes you think I'm not going to tell Mom about this?" I didn't bother keeping my voice low. I waited for the explosion that usually comes when I threaten my sister. She smiled and said nothing, which kind of freaked me out. "Well?" I tried to sound intimidating rather than confused.

"I figure we both owe Justin after today."

I kept my mouth shut, and Captain William seemed subdued. It was crazy to think that I owed her stupid boyfriend anything. He was the one who was dating *my* sister. He was the one with blue hair. He was the one who had the nerve to call my sister Tina. I folded my arms across my chest, afraid now that I was going to be the one to explode.

"Think about it," Kristina said. "If Justin hadn't come and gotten us, we would've had to wait until like one in the morning for the next low tide. Mom would've freaked. She probably would've called the police."

"And she would've been very happy when we turned up fine," I pointed out.

"Yeah. And when she got over that, she would've grounded us forever."

Kristina was right. We probably wouldn't have figured out another way off the island if Justin hadn't come to pick us up. He had kept both of us from getting in a lot of trouble.

"Fine," I said. "But Andy's having dinner with us, too."

I technically didn't have permission to have Andy over for dinner, but he ate with us all the time and was allowed in the house when my parents weren't home. Having Andy over without asking wasn't nearly as bad as sneaking Justin into the house behind my parents' backs.

"That's fine with me." She strolled past me and went back into the living room. I slowly followed. Justin was actually looking at the menu this time.

"We were thinking Chinese," Kristina said. "Justin and I can pick it up. What do you and Andy like?"

"Kung Pao chicken." That was what we always ordered. "And get us fried rice."

I stayed in the living room and flicked through the TV channels. There was nothing on, but I wasn't going to leave the two lovebirds alone. They didn't kiss or anything, but they did hold hands the whole time. It kind of made me sick to my stomach; maybe I shouldn't have ordered something so spicy.

Andy rode up on his bike just as Kristina and Lover Boy were about to leave. "My dad couldn't give me a ride. Do you think your parents could bring me home later?"

"Uh, I guess." I hadn't really planned on telling my parents about him coming over, but I guessed they wouldn't be too mad.

Kristina interrupted, "Justin can give you a ride home. Right, Babe?"

"Yeah, sure," Justin said.

My pirate blood boiled under my skin. "No. Mom won't mind."

"Forget about it," Kristina said with a pointed look. "There's no need for Mom to find out that we had guests for dinner. Justin will bring Andy home," she lowered her voice, "or I'll tell Mom what you've been up to. End of story."

That was just what I needed: Lover Boy doing another favor for me. But I also didn't need my mom finding out about our little adventure on Pirate Island. Kristina would find a way to spin it so it looked like all my fault. "Fine."

"Justin may be a future rock star, but he's really such a sweetheart." She kissed Justin on the cheek, and Andy pretended to gag behind them. Then they finally went to pick up the food.

"I'm starving," Andy said. "What's for dinner?"

"Kung Pao."

"Awesome. Hey, check this out." Andy pulled a book out of his backpack and grinned. "Ahoy me matey," he said in a gruff voice. "Get yeeself to the poop deck and fetch me some grog."

I had no idea what he was talking about, but that didn't stop me from having a good comeback. "Get yer own self to the poop deck. But I sure don't want you to fetch me anything from there."

We cracked up. It was great to have my best friend back. No, it was better than great; it was awesome. (And ultimately short-lived.)

Chapter 29

Andy flipped through the book, which had a million ways to talk like a pirate. "Grog is a pirate drink. And the poop deck is part of a ship. My mom sent it to me."

"Cool," I said. It seemed to be more how a person imagines a pirate would talk than how they actually talked back in the days of pirates. Given that, fake pirate talk had its uses. "Maybe we can insult Justin without him knowing it."

"Definitely. There's a whole section of insults. Oh, and look, here's another one on threats."

I reached for the book. "Let me see."

Andy pulled it to his chest. "Wait, I wasn't kidding about the grog. We can't have Kung Pao without drinks."

I got a couple of sodas out of the kitchen. On a whim, I ran to my room and pulled out the pirate costume and brought it to the living room. Andy had the book open on the coffee table. When he noticed the costume, he called dibs on the hat and hook, so I got stuck with the eye patch and too-small vest.

He turned back to the book. "Here's a good threat. I'll squeeze yer squeezy cheese-head off yer body. Or how about this insult? There is more of life in me little finger than in all yee carcass."

"Ha," I said. "Alright, my turn."

I grabbed the book off the table and brought it to the couch. Andy starting yammering on about football, gesturing with his hook hand every so often. Less than a week had gone by since we'd last talked, but a lot had happened with his team. I tried to listen, but the pirate talk was much more interesting.

I had a fake-pirate-talk toast prepared when Kristina and Lover Boy got back from the Chinese place. I wouldn't let them open their food until I said it.

I tried to make my voice sound gruff and threatening, like how Kidd would have sounded when addressing his crew. "To success on arr ventures. To fortunate preeceedin's an' gooder friendship. Let us drain a garrblet, clink cannerkin an' toss a pot ter thar great makees of Chinese grub. Drink arrp, me hearties, yo ho!"

"William," Kristina said. "You're such a dork."

I was about to call her a bilge-sucking, cutthroat tarrmagant when Andy cut in with, "William, like Captain William Kidd? What happened to Billy?"

He was close to making fun of me, that much I could tell, so I threw his own words from our fight right back at him. "I decided Billy is a name for a *little kid*."

If we were truly going to be friends again, Andy was going to have to learn that he couldn't boss me around anymore. And I would have to learn to keep Captain William, whose blood boiled in anger again, in check.

He shrugged and said, "Okay, William."

I let his agreement be good enough for me to move on.

We spent most of dinner searching through the book. I ditched the eye patch because it made it hard to read, and hard to aim food at my mouth. In between mouthfuls of Kung Pao, we came up with as many insults for Kristina and Justin as we could. At first they ignored us, but after a while we started getting on their nerves.

"Hey, Kris," I said. "Yarr a hen-hearted curmudgeon."

"Hey, Justin," Andy said. "Why don't ya use yarr swivel-tongued mouth ter scrape thee barnacles off thee poop deck."

We practically fell off the couch laughing.

"Justin," Kristina said. "Do you have any idea what these boys are saying?"

With a forkful of food poised in front of his mouth, he looked back and forth between us and Kristina. He took her not so subtle hint. "Uh, no."

"In that case," she said. "We should just assume that everything they say is a compliment. So, thank you very much, William."

"Yeah," Justin said. "Thanks."

They stuck to thanking us every time we tried to

insult them, so we soon gave up. The lovebirds had managed to take the fun out of it. The four of us sat around watching TV for another hour before Justin and Andy had to leave.

I watched from the window as Kristina said good-bye to her boyfriend. Andy sat in the front seat, his eyes staring straight ahead. I tried to look away, but I just couldn't. It was like my eyeballs were glued in place, forcing me to watch the disgusting shipwreck that was my sister and her boyfriend.

Holding hands, they moved closer to each other, and then Justin put his hand behind Kristina's head. Oh, gross! What was wrong with me? Why was I watching this? I finally managed to clap my hands over my eyes before anything else happened. I turned my head, uncovered my eyes, and ran back to the living room.

Kristina's cheeks were all pink when she sat down next to me a few minutes later. "So I guess you and Andy kissed and made up."

How could she talk to me about kissing? "Gross. I'm going upstairs."

Chapter 30

Later that night, a knock at the door interrupted my latest read through of the stack of papers and books about the island and Captain Kidd. I was surprised to see my mom because I hadn't heard my parents get home.

"Hi, Billy," she said. I wanted to correct her by saying "William" but didn't. "How was dinner?"

"Good," I said. "I had Kung Pao."

"Did you get your phone messages?"

"Oh, yeah. I already talked to Andy."

"So you two finally made up?"

I nodded. "Yup."

My mom patted me on the shoulder. She probably wanted more information, but that was all I needed to say on the topic.

I thought she was going to press the issue but instead asked, "Who's Eleanor Birch?"

"Who?" I asked.

"Eleanor Birch," my mom repeated.

I stared at her. She probably thought I was being

really dumb. Then again, I was feeling really dumb.

"Didn't you see her message?" she asked.

"Um, no."

She handed me a slip of paper. I had totally forgotten that there had been a second phone message for me. I guess I had been too worked up over Andy's. I unfolded the paper. It said Eleanor Birch had changed her mind and would talk to me about the matter we had discussed in our previous phone call. Why was that name familiar?

My mom moved to the doorway but waited for me to explain. My gaze wandered over the stack of Pirate Island stuff. The pamphlet Kristina had given me poked out the side of the pile. Oh, right...crazy old lady who thought the island was "thrice cursed."

"She's from the historical society," I said. "I had called her about some research for my writing class, but she didn't have very much information." The lie slipped out easily.

My mom kissed me on the forehead and told me to get ready for bed. I brought Eleanor Birch's message into the bathroom and reread it while I brushed my teeth. So she wanted to talk about Pirate Island. I should've been really happy. Andy was my best friend again, and he wanted to look for Kidd's treasure. Eleanor Birch might give us an actual lead.

So why did my stomach feel queasy? Maybe it was the Kung Pao. Or maybe it was almost seeing my sister and Lover Boy kiss. I told myself that was all it was, the spicy food and my sister and her gross boyfriend.

(Little did I know my insides hurt over the war being waged inside myself. A war over my soul. One I hope to win on Pirate Island tonight.)

Chapter 31

The morning after Andy and I returned to our status as best friends, I called Eleanor Birch. The phone was on its seventh ring and I was about to hang up when someone finally answered.

"Hello?" the voice on the other end said.

"Uh, hi," I said. "This is William Bonny. I'm calling for Eleanor Birch."

"Yes, this is Eleanor." Her voice wavered and crackled like there was static on the line, but I knew it was only because she was ancient. "Who are you?"

"William Bonny," I said loudly into the phone. "I called you about Pirate Island and you didn't want to talk about it, but you called me back yesterday and left a message that said you would talk about it."

There was silence on the other line. I was blathering again. Like I said, the phone isn't a strong point for me. Another moment of silence passed, and I wondered if I should say anything.

"Oh, yes," she said. "William, dearie. I remember now.

Pirate Island. My neighbor found out you called, and I told her what I said to you about the curses. She said I shouldn't have tried to scare you and that I should talk with you. Would you like to come over this afternoon?"

Today? That was too soon. I needed more time to prepare. Plus, what if she was a kidnapper? I didn't want to go walking into a crazy lady's house all by myself. Still, just two days ago I had lost all hope of finding Kidd's treasure. Eleanor Birch could be the clue we had been looking for all along, the one thing that could tell us exactly where the loot was buried.

(That is, except for Kidd, but so far he'd only communicated through pirate rage and an attempt at drowning me. This whole thing would have been a lot easier if he told me where the treasure was. But he wasn't—still isn't—so Eleanor Birch was my best lead.)

"Fine." My voice cracked this time, or maybe there really was static on the line. Earlier I had been outside, and the summer air hung heavy with pending thunderstorms. That could cause phone disruptions, right? "I'll come by this afternoon."

After I got off the phone, I ran down the hall to Kristina's bedroom. I explained to her about going to Eleanor Birch's house. "Please, please, please come with me."

"Ugh," she said. "Aren't you ever going to get over this pirate-treasure thing? Can't Andy go with you instead?"

"No and no," I said. "I'm not going to get over this whole pirate-treasure thing, and Andy has football. Don't make me tell Mom about your boyfriend being over last night."

Kristina wrapped her arms around my neck and pulled me to the ground. She twisted my arms behind my back and pinned me with her knee. With my face mashed into the rug and my ears ringing, I could hardly breathe. For someone so unathletic, my sister sure was quick, and strong.

"I'm so sick of you threatening me all the time." Her voice was muffled but firm. I flailed my arms, trying to free them from her freakishly strong grasp, but she held tight.

"Lumme gha," I said with a mouthful of rug.

"What?" her knee lightened its hold on me a little.

"Let me go."

"Are you going to keep threatening me?"

I didn't answer right away. Captain William didn't like being forced into anything, but I think he (I...I'm Captain William) saw there wasn't much choice in this situation.

Kristina pushed down her knee again and with her hand, smushed my face right back into the rug. It was like she had been practicing with the wrestling team. I managed to squeak out a noise of reply, which must've sounded like a no because she lessened the pressure on my back.

"Was that a no?" she asked.

"Yes," I said.

Her hand twitched behind my head. "It was a yes?"

"No, it was a yes that it was a no."

"Don't be smart with me, William. Answer the question. Are you going to keep threatening me?"

"No!"

"Okay, now we're getting somewhere."

She took her knee off my back and helped me up. She pointed to her desk chair. "Sit."

I crossed my arms over my chest. "I'm not a dog."

"Do you want my help?"

I nodded.

"Then sit down," she said.

"Fine." I sat in the chair. She'd better not try to pull a smoke-and-mirrors act on me. She paced the length of her bed. "So I know you and Andy were fighting, and I've been trying to be nice to you and all, but do you really think you're gonna find pirate treasure?"

"Why not. It's called Pirate Island for a reason. And I think Eleanor Birch almost found Captain Kidd's treasure there. Please come with me this afternoon. I can't let this chance go by, and I'm kind of scared to go by myself."

Andy wasn't the only person who knew how to get what he wanted. If my sister thought I was scared (okay, and I was a little scared), maybe she would take pity on me. She stopped pacing.

"C'mon," I said. "You can wait to hang out with Justin until after we get back, right?"

"Hey! You called him Justin." She stared at me for a minute. "He *is* rehearsing with the band this afternoon. You're really set on seeing this through?"

I opened my eyes wide and nodded with my best puppy-dog face.

"Alright," she said. "I'll come with you."

"Yes!" I yelled. "Meet me downstairs in twenty minutes."

I jumped out of the chair and ran to my room to gather my materials. I wanted to make sure I was prepared with any questions that might help us. I had a feeling that Eleanor Birch was one of the only people in the world who could tell us how to find Kidd's treasure.

Chapter 32

The inside of Eleanor Birch's house was pretty much how I expected it to be: dark, musty, and hideously ugly. The kitchen had poop-brown cabinets and a puke-green refrigerator. What kind of person decorates with colors based on bodily functions? And it was really warm in there, like being thrown into a hot volcano.

Ms. Birch led us to a porch-like room in the back of the house that my mom would've called a sunroom. It was sunny outside, but it was definitely not bright on that porch. Dark curtains hung around the windows, and dust floated through the air. It was even warmer back there than in the rest of the house. Hadn't this lady ever heard of air conditioning? One look at Kristina's narrowed eyes and pursed lips told me she was hating every inch of me for dragging her there.

"Sit, dearies." Ms. Birch pointed to a table and folding chairs. "Would you like some tea?"

"Tea?" Kristina said. "Isn't it a little warm for tea?"

I hoped she wouldn't lose it before we got started.

"Lemonade, then?" Ms. Birch asked.

"Yes," I said before Kristina could be rude again. "Please."

"Sit and get comfortable, then, dearies. I'll just be a minute."

The chair's hard metal dug into my back, but at least it was cool. Kristina settled into hers and practically breathed fire at me. My armpits were drenched in sweat. Where was the air conditioner in the library's conference room when I need it? I would gladly let Ella Platt witness my gorilla act, so long as I could cool off.

"I can't believe you made me come here," Kristina said.

"Be nice. She might have information for us."

"Us? This is *your* crazy project. You're the one who thinks there's buried treasure."

I squirmed in my seat. "Fine. She has information for me. Please, be nice. You promised you'd help."

She threw her hands up. "Okay, okay. I'll be nice."

I would've actually thanked Kristina, but Ms. Birch was back. She set down a tray with glasses and a pitcher of pink lemonade. Then she headed to a corner of the room where there was a medium-sized box and bent to pick it up.

"Wait," Kristina said loudly. "I'll carry it."

"Thank you, dear," Ms. Birch said as she sat. "What did you say your name was?"

"Kristina."

"Kristina what?"

My sister froze halfway back to the table, box in her arms. "Excuse me?"

"Do you have a last name?"

Kristina breathed more fire in my direction. "It's Bonny." She thunked the box onto the table. I took a sip of lemonade as my throat was suddenly very dry.

"Bonny," Ms. Birch said. "That's a good pirate name. Anne Bonny was a famous pirate, and a woman to boot."

I didn't want to be rude, but we were getting off topic. "We came here to talk about Captain William Kidd."

"Right, dearie." She rifled through the contents of the box and pulled out a fat folder. "Captain Kidd. He was an evil man. Greedy too. He abandoned his wife and young daughters to be a pirate. And for what? Fine silk, expensive spices, gold. He traded respect and love for possessions. His life is as an example of how not to live."

I didn't agree with her opinion of Kidd (and neither did he), but we kept our mouths shut. We weren't there to argue with her but to find out if she knew where the loot was buried.

"I was fascinated by him as a misguided young woman," Ms. Birch said. "Young ladies are so often taken in by greed and immorality."

She looked right at Kristina, whose face turned red. The room was hot enough already without Ms. Birch stoking the fire that burned within my sister.

"But what about Pirate Island and Captain Kidd's treasure?" I asked.

"Patience, dearie," she said. "So it's Pirate Island you want to talk about. You should know about the curses then."

She flipped through the folder and pulled out several papers. She looked at them in silence. When she finally spoke, it was in a low voice. "Pirate Island and most of this town were originally owned by the Paugusset Indian tribe, headed by Chief Ansantawae. They sold all their land to English settlers for a few trinkets. The Paugusset tribe soon realized their mistake. In particular, the tribe considered Pirate Island sacred land. After losing it, Chief Ansantawae cursed it with these words…"

Ms. Birch paused and her voice got real deep. "*Any man who dares break ground on this island shall be cursed, and any shelter there raised shall crumble to the Earth.*"

It was very quiet. I wouldn't have been surprised to hear thunder in the distance, but outside the sun innocently shone though the haze. Goose bumps peppered my arms, despite all the sweating.

"The chief's curse has turned out to be true enough, as no building has lasted very long on the island," she said. "And then there was that Mexican emperor. Let's see, what was his name?"

She rifled through the folder again. "Ah, yes. Emperor Guatmozin. His curse wasn't placed directly on Pirate Island, but nevertheless it ended up there. The Emperor was a wealthy man but a greedy man too. He hid his riches in a cave in Mexico and placed a curse on his treasure chest such that anyone who opened it would die a very painful death. Five sailors found it and decided to bring it home. One man died on the journey. One-by-one the other men perished, until there was only a single man left. In a final effort to save his own life, he buried the chest on Pirate Island. His fate had already been sealed, though, and within a month he was dead."

Now I was really expecting to hear thunder, or maybe a great swoosh as the ghost of that emperor swooped down on us, but the only noise was a dog barking in the distance.

"And that brings us to Kidd. A privateer turned pirate." Ms. Birch looked first at me and then at Kristina, reproach in her gaze. "As a young woman, I thought his life was romantic and tragic. But it was treacherous, and his curse was the worst of them all."

My hand twitched on my thigh. I wanted to slap those words right out of her mouth. I dug my fingernails into my palm to keep still. It was seriously messed up to have the urge to hit an old lady. Patience, I told Kidd, this old lady might finally give us some answers.

Chapter 33

Neither Kristina nor I (nor Kidd) said a word as Ms. Birch kept on talking. "I'm getting ahead of myself. My brother was equally as transfixed with Captain Kidd. We spent a great deal of a long-ago summer researching all we could about the pirate. We found this letter from one young resident named Patience Tuttle."

Patience Tuttle. The name sparked a tiny flame in my memory, but I couldn't place it.

Ms. Birch set a yellowed, crumbling letter on the table for us to read.

Aunt Prudence has told you of ye visit from Captain
Kidd, from ye craft wh. was seen to come in ye harbor
at 7 of ye clock in ye evening. He stayed in ye house
till in ye early morning, and sat all ye night by ye fire
with Jacobeth and Thomas Welsh carrying himself in
an uncivil and bold manner.

It went on about Kidd's bad behavior a bit more before one last interesting bit.

I overheard Jacobeth say yt Kidd was going on a long

cruise, and yt he had left some things with him.

None of the books or articles had put him specifically in my hometown, but this letter—which I had never read—did. So hearing the name Patience Tuttle must have sparked something in Kidd, not me.

My skin prickled with excitement. "What kind of things did Captain Kidd leave with Jacobeth?"

"I don't know," she said. "But the letter caused me and my brother a good deal of excitement. We were sure Kidd had given Jacobeth instructions on how to find Kidd's buried treasure. We tried to track down the ancestors of Patience and Jacobeth, but we never found any. We did find another little piece of intrigue, though, an entry in Jacobeth's diary."

She pulled yet another piece of paper from her gold-mine of a folder. It was brown, very wrinkled, and torn in several places. It looked like it might fall apart at any moment. She also set that on the table for us to read:

met Kidd outside ye harbor on a grand ship. I's
assisted him in depositing 7 iron boxes to ye island, ye
contents of which were gold and silver coin, and
jewells, and jems. Ye likes of which I had never laid
ye...

The rest of the letter had torn off. My legs bounced in excitement. It took all of my resolve not to get up and dance around the room. Kidd's mind was becoming clearer to me. Images flashed in my brain: men digging, giant boxes being

160

lowered into the ground, sailing away from Pirate Island. Was Kidd finally letting me in on his memories of where the treasure was?

Ms. Birch's voice interrupted my (our?) thoughts. "Unfortunately there was only one other page with the diary entry, and it was blank. My brother and I eventually gave up looking for the treasure."

She stared out the window but didn't seem to be looking at anything in particular, like how Mrs. Shields had looked when she told me about her visit to Pirate Island. Did every old person have a crazy story about the island?

"I was nearly a woman when Kidd's story entered my life again," she continued. "A beau of mine escorted me to Pirate Island for a picnic. He told me he had heard of the treasure. I suppose he wanted to impress me. I confessed that I had once believed in the treasure myself. Oh, I was such a foolish young woman."

She stared down Kristina, as if her gaze could break down all the foolishness that must reside inside of my sister. Kristina pushed back her chair, but I grabbed her arm before she could stand.

I had to know the end of this story. It was jogging loose the pieces I needed—we needed—to find the treasure. I summoned good-boy Billy and did my best impression of a needy puppy dog, holding just short of whimpering. Kristina shot me a deadly glare but stayed seated. She was going to kill me.

"Ms. Birch," I said. "What about Captain Kidd's treasure? Did you ever end up looking for it?"

"Yes," she said. "Yes, we did."

She was silent for what felt like forever. I was trying to think of what to say when Kristina spoke up in a surprisingly soft voice. "Ms. Birch? What happened out there on Pirate Island?"

"It was the worst night of my life." Her voice was so low, I almost couldn't hear it. "I don't like to talk about it. That's why I didn't want to talk to you at first, dearies."

"Well, William and I are thinking of going to Pirate Island to look for Kidd's treasure," Kristina said.

I kicked her under the table, but she mouthed the words "trust me."

Then she said, "You telling us what happened will help us make a decision on whether or not to go there."

I held my breath, waiting to see if Ms. Birch would respond.

She did in that same quiet voice. "My young suitor— George was his name—piqued my interest in finding Kidd's treasure. I showed him all the research we had done. George was fascinated. He borrowed the papers. He was a very intelligent young man. That was one of the things that had attracted me to him. He found a secret message that led us right to the treasure. Oh, how I wish he never had."

Thunder cracked outside. We all jumped in our seats. The sky had turned an odd shade of bluish green that matched the waters of Long Island Sound. A storm was rolling in. Outside, a bright flash of lightning sliced through the clouds. I almost slipped off my cold, metal chair.

Kristina jumped out of her seat and peered out the window. "Whoa. Those are some serious looking clouds."

Another boom punctuated her words.

"Oh, dear," Ms. Birch said. "All the windows are open. We don't want it to rain on our lemonade."

I snorted in an attempt to hold back my laughter. "Don't you mean rain on our parade?"

"Never mind that," Kristina said. "We'll help. William, get all the windows in here closed."

The two of them left to close off the rest of the house. The windows in the sunroom were old crank ones, and it took some real muscle to get each one closed. By the time I had finished, rain was pouring down at an angle. The wind whipped the leaves on the trees upside down. Kristina and Ms. Birch returned.

Lightning flashed every few minutes. I counted to five before the thunder rolled, meaning the center of the storm was one mile away. No matter how close, the storm wasn't top in my mind because Ms. Birch had been about to tell us something important, and Kidd's mind felt closer than ever to mine.

Chapter 34

Ignoring the storm outside, I (and Kidd) focused on Eleanor Birch.

"Ms. Birch," I said after she and Kristina sat back down. "Can you please tell us about that night on Pirate Island?"

She rubbed her hands together. "Patience is a stir brew, dearie."

"What?" I shook my head in confusion. Was she speaking in fake pirate talk?

"She means patience is a virtue," Kristina said. "We're waiting patiently, Ms. Birch."

"I will tell you," she said. "If only to keep you far away from that cursed island. We—my brother, George, and I—went to Pirate Island on a hot summer night. We followed the instructions George had found and began to dig. Hours went by and nothing. My brother was very angry. He never approved of George, thought he was too much of an intellectual. I don't remember anymore who pushed who first, but pretty soon they were on the ground wrestling.

They rolled and George fell into the hole, hitting his head on the bottom."

The storm was in full swing outside, but we were dead still in the room. Ms. Birch's voice was barely a whisper. "When he stood, blood covered the side of his face and shirt. I think the sight of the blood brought my brother to his senses. The hole was higher than George could reach, so my brother crouched down and reached over to help him. I held the light above them. My brother had his arms under George's armpits and was about to pull him over the edge when a single drop of blood dripped off his head and landed in the dirt."

Outside lightning flashed and thunder cracked almost simultaneously. Wind and rain pounded the windows. The worst of the storm was on top of us, but I didn't care. I had to know what happened to George.

Ms. Birch stood and swayed back and forth with her eyes closed, like she was in a trance. This wasn't the same frail, old lady we had met at the door. She was shouting now. "Blue light surrounded us! There was a terrible noise —like the screeching brakes of a train combined with a boiling teakettle. I'd never been so terrified in all my life. At first I was frozen by the light. It was my life, my world, all that I knew in that moment!"

She sank into her seat, her voice the croak of an old lady again. "I don't know how long I stayed still, a second, a week, a lifetime. A hand grabbed mine, the only warmth in the chill of blue light. It broke the spell. The light disappeared. The hand pulled me across the sandbar and off the island. I was now blinded by darkness and couldn't see who gripped my hand, and feared for the one who didn't. We reached the beach, and with the little bit of moonlight, I saw the survivor."

The storm had faded to the trickle of rain and the distant rumble of thunder.

"Who was it?" Kristina whispered.

"My brother. And I was ashamed to be so relieved. I was stricken with guilt to be happy that my brother and I had escaped the island, while George was..."

She rested her face in her hands and sobbed. I had never seen a grown up cry like that. When she finally calmed down, she pulled a wrinkled tissue from her sleeve, blew her nose, and stuck the tissue back in her sleeve. It was pretty gross. I tried not to gag while Kristina poured Ms. Birch a glass of lemonade and insisted she drink it.

"I'm sorry, dearies," Ms. Birch continued. "This is very difficult for me. Where was I?"

"Your brother pulled you off the island," I said. "You were about to tell us what happened to George."

She sniffled. "Of course. George was, well, we really don't know what George was. He was lost. They called him a missing person. He was never found and the police closed the case."

"What do you mean the police closed the case?"

Kristina asked. "How could they close the case?"

"There was no evidence. We ran straight to the police station. They searched the island all the next day and found nothing. No shovels, no light, no sign of the hole we had dug. No George, not even a body. They drove us back to the station and interrogated us for hours. We told them the truth. They didn't believe us. They figured we had gone there to party and that George had gotten drunk and gone out in the water and drowned."

Ms. Birch let out a big sigh, her body sagging like a deflated balloon. "They kept the case open for a few years. It was a sensation. No one blamed us for what happened. They wanted to know the truth. What could we tell them? I stopped talking and let them all believe what they wanted. Eventually the excitement died down and people began to forget about the incident. Not my brother, though. I think he blamed himself for George's disappearance."

Her voice had gone hoarse. She took another sip of lemonade. Her eyes stared at nothing, and she was silent for a while. Kristina gently touched her hand. "Where's your brother now?"

"Dead," she said. The storm had waned, and the chirping of cicadas filled in where the rain and thunder had left off. "He spent most of his adult life in a halfway house. He suffered from terrible nightmares. Like me, he never married. Neither of us ever felt the same after that night on Pirate Island. Some pieces of the puzzle had gone missing and, like George, were never found. We could never put our lives back together. He went to bed two nights before his fifty-fourth birthday and never woke up. I'd like to think that he finally rests in peace."

Ms. Birch's story—her real-life story—was getting way too heavy for me. I didn't want to hear any more about the sadness Pirate Island had caused her.

"You now understand why you must never go looking for Kidd's treasure," she said. "It's too dangerous...deadly!"

I didn't know what to say to that. What had happened to George on Pirate Island was terrible, but that didn't mean it would happen to us. Surely our own adventure wouldn't turn out so sad. We would be more careful. We had Kidd on our side, though his presence had subsided deep within me.

"You must be very tired, Ms. Birch," Kristina said. "Is there anything we can get you before we leave?"

"No. Thank you, dearies," she said.

"Thank you for sharing your story," I found myself saying. But I wasn't ready to leave, not without the concrete evidence they had used to find out where to dig for the treasure. My brain was working overtime trying to figure out how to get it.

"Oh, maybe there is one thing you can do for me," Ms. Birch said. "Make me a promise. A promise that you'll never dig on Pirate Island."

That was one thing I couldn't promise her. Her story

was tragic, but a young man doesn't disappear like that for nothing. It (and Kidd's stirrings in my mind) convinced me that Pirate Island needed to be searched.

"Don't worry about us," Captain William said. "We promise we'll stay safe."

I had every intention of staying safe, so there was no lie there. I nodded, having found a way to satisfy both William and good-boy Billy.

Ms. Birch didn't seem to notice my duplicitous promise. On a whim, I offered to put away the box of Pirate Island materials. I was happy to stick them in the back of her living room closet like she asked. I thanked her a final time as she shut the door behind Kristina and me.

"Well, that was a crazy story," Kristina said as we walked home. The sun was back out, though much lower in the sky than when we had set out. A couple of small puddles and a few green leaves littered the sidewalk, the only signs that a huge storm had raged through town. "Too bad it didn't help you much in figuring out where to dig."

"Not necessarily," I said slowly.

"What are you saying?" She eyed me with suspicion.

I pulled a yellowed, crumpled scrap of paper from my back pocket. It was the blank page from Jacobeth's journal. I had snatched it out of the box before putting it away.

"William," Kristina said. "Did you steal that from Ms. Birch?"

"Not technically. I plan on returning it."

"That's great and all, but it's blank. What good is it?"

"I think it's a treasure map. I just have to figure out how to use it."

"Wow." She seemed equal parts impressed and scandalized. "I didn't think you had it in you to be a thief." I started to say I wasn't a thief—that I was going to return the page when I was done with it—but Kristina kept on talking, "Don't get me wrong. I'm kind of impressed. Maybe you do have what it takes to be a pirate."

I grinned. I was willing to borrow (okay, more likely steal because when was I going to get a chance to return the page?) from Ms. Birch because we were closer than ever to finding Kidd's treasure. I couldn't wait to call Andy and tell him what I had discovered.

Chapter 35

The minute I arrived home, I grabbed the phone and headed to my room, intending to call Andy to tell him the news. But as my finger hovered over the numbers, something (an impulse from Kidd?) stopped me.

Now that I was so close to finding the treasure, why should I share it with Andy? Before our fight, he hadn't really helped at all. I had done all the work. Kristina—and Justin—had contributed along the way, much more than Andy had.

I tossed the phone onto my bed and started up my computer. Kidd's presence was dormant for the time being, but I could figure out how to reveal the mystery of the blank page from Jacobeth's journal all on my own.

I spent most of the next 24 hours researching hidden messages. My mom thought I was working on my ghost story for the summer writing class, so she let me be.

On Monday night, I hastily typed up an ending to my story, which was due the next morning. Andy was already in our usual seats in the back when I got there. Ella was in the front, surrounded by her usual gaggle of girls.

She smiled when I walked by, but I hardly noticed. Silly ghost stories weren't important, and neither were girls. Not when I had a treasure to find.

I was kind of mad at Kidd, who hadn't shown up once since revealing those images at Ms. Birch's house of his crew burying the treasure on Pirate Island. If only he would pop into my mind and tell me exactly where the treasure was, we could end this. But he was as silent as the stinkiest SBD—silent but deadly—fart.

There was hardly time for a quick hello before Mrs. Shields started class, so I didn't have to worry about Andy asking about the treasure hunt. I hardly paid attention, slipping Andy's one-page submission under my thick story when it was time to turn them in to be made into a "real" book for the last class next week.

We were given one short writing prompt to work on for the first half of class, and the second half was devoted to planning the end-of-class party. I rested my hand on my head and actually dozed off for a bit. Before I knew it, class was over.

Andy followed me to the door, but I shrugged him off, telling him I had to get home for a family thing. I hopped on my bike, which I hadn't bothered to chain to the rack, and pedaled home as fast as I could.

At home, I jumped in the pool to clean off the sweat from the ride home and allowed myself a half-hour of TV, which turned into a nap that lasted until dinner. The lack of sleep must have finally caught up with me, but I returned to my research with renewed energy that night.

Kidd continued to elude me, but Captain William pushed through.

By Wednesday morning, I had concluded that Kidd must've written on the page with invisible ink. I discovered that there were all types of regular things that could be used as invisible ink, like lemon juice, vinegar, and milk. The weirdest was definitely pee. Sure, in the winter I had written my name in the snow, but to write a secret message with pee was pretty gross.

The bottom line was that even in the 17th century, Kidd would've had access to most of those things. And it didn't matter so much what he used but how to discover what he had written.

Lots of invisible-ink messages could be revealed if you put the paper up to a heat source, but once a message was revealed it stayed visible. Seeing as the page was blank, I figured Ms. Birch hadn't used that method.

It was time to test out the theory I had developed about how to reveal the paper's secret. All it took was a few dollars and a trip to the hardware store to get the materials. Unfortunately, Andy was waiting for me outside my house when I got home.

"Your mom said I could wait here," he said when I pulled up on my bike.

With Kidd missing in action and Andy performing his old smoke-and-mirrors routine by showing up uninvited, I caved and told him all about Ms. Birch, her crazy story, Patience Tuttle's letter about Kidd's visit to town, and Jacobeth's journal.

"It's just an old, blank piece of paper," he said about the journal page I had stolen from Ms. Birch.

"Yes, it's a piece of paper, and yes, it's old," I said. "But it's not blank."

Andy flipped his hair. "It sure looks blank to me."

I wanted to ring his neck. And then the strangest thing happened, my own neck twinged. I held in a gasp. Kidd was back!

"Looks can be deceiving," I said, knowing he wouldn't suspect me of being deceitful. "I think it has a secret message on it. If we can figure out how to read it, it's jackpot for us."

"Okay. Then how do we do that?"

I pulled my hardware purchase out of a paper bag.

"A light bulb?" Andy said.

"Not just any light bulb. A black light bulb."

I'm not sure why it's called a black light because it's actually purple. Didn't matter, so long as it did the job. I unplugged my desk lamp and switched out the regular one for the black (purple) one. I plugged the lamp back in and turned off all the lights in the room.

I hesitated; this was the moment of truth, and I

couldn't click the switch. What if it didn't work?

In the darkness, Kidd whispered in my head. *Andy's not a true believer. He abandoned you and the treasure. He doesn't deserve the riches. Only you do.*

"What are you waiting for?" Andy demanded.

With a deliberate flick of the wrist, I knocked over the desk lamp. It crashed to the carpet and the light bulb exploded into a million tiny pieces. I shouted in surprise to make Andy think it was an accident.

I turned on the overhead light. "Sorry. I'll have to get another one."

"We can go now," Andy said. "We'll take our bikes."

I looked at the clock on my nightstand. "I have soccer practice soon." Not true. My practice was the next night. "You should go. I have to get ready."

I walked him to the front door, practically pushing him out.

"I'll come over tomorrow, and we'll take a trip to the hardware store," Andy said as he mounted his bike.

"Sure," I said. "I'll call you."

I watched him pedal down the road. As soon as he was out of sight, I hopped back on my bike and took another ride to the hardware store.

It would be wrong to say I rode alone; I was never alone anymore. Kidd was here to stay.

Chapter 36

With a new black light screwed into my desk lamp, I turned it on and held the blank page from Ms. Birch's house up close to it. I gasped, the paper shaking in my hand.

A map glowed in the light. There was an island in the exact shape of Pirate Island. The tombolo was there, represented by a strip of land trailing off the north side of the island. Several circles adorned the east side of the island, dotted lines extending off two of them. Next to one dotted line it read in a fancy hand-written script *62 P*, and next to the other was a fancy *66 P*.

"Sixty-two P," I said. "What could that mean?" I repeated P to myself over and over again until I heard a giggle from behind my closed door.

When my eyes adjusted to the bright hallway light, I found Kristina holding her stomach and laughing.

"Pee, pee, pee," she said. "If you gotta go, you know where the bathroom is."

I dragged her into my room and slammed the door shut. Without saying anything, I held the map up to the black light.

"No way!" she squealed. Then her voice turned to a whisper, "Is this for real?"

I nodded and crossed my heart with a finger.

"Seriously," she said. "You're not making this up?"

"No way. This is the page I borrowed from Eleanor Birch."

"So all we have to do is walk sixty-two and sixty-six paces from those rocks and where they meet up is where the treasure is buried?"

A very bright light bulb went off in my head. "Wait. Paces. That's what the P's stand for. You're a genius, Kristina!"

She squealed again. "Seriously, Billy—I mean William. This means we might actually be able to find the treasure. I mean, I thought you were crazy to think that Captain Kidd buried treasure on Pirate Island, but this is the real thing. When do we go?"

She was dead serious, and excited! That's when I realized how huge this was.

I was about to check when the next full moon was when our mom yelled that dinner was ready.

I didn't exactly pay attention to the dinner conversation. It felt like my chair was electrified and the current was running up my spine and into my neck. Or maybe that was Kidd buzzing away with excitement, like I was.

As soon as my plate was empty, I ran to the computer. Kristina was right behind me. The next full moon was Friday, and low tide was at 6:47 pm. I looked at my sister, her face flush with excitement.

Kidd whispered in my head, an ivy vine tickling my ear, planting its poison.

Don't trust her. She wants it for herself.

I coughed to drown him out. If anyone deserved to be on Pirate Island when I found the treasure, it was Kristina. And in less than 48 hours, we would be there, paces away from Kidd's buried treasure.

"We can't tell Andy," I said, at least I think it was me. It was so hard to tell who was doing the talking at this point.

"He's your best friend," Kristina said. "He should know. He should be there."

"Promise me you won't tell him, and I'll let you bring Justin along." Anything to keep Andy out of the picture.

She crossed her heart, and that was all the reassurance I needed.

A tingle around my neck let me know Kidd wasn't exactly happy with the situation, but I was growing tired of his demands. I was having nightmares about almost drowning on the tombolo; the least he could do was cater to some of my demands. Kristina was coming to Pirate Island.

Chapter 37

Kristina and I came up with a plan for the night we would go to Pirate Island. I would tell my mom that I was sleeping over Andy's, and Kristina would tell her she was sleeping at her friend's house. We would meet at the beach a half hour before low tide so we would have plenty of time to walk out to the island.

Thursday ticked by second-by-second. It was like it was the day before Christmas and I had nothing to do but stare at the slow progress of the second hand for the entire 24 hours.

When Friday evening finally arrived, my mom gave me a ride to Andy's. She let me bring my bike, which was secured on the bike rack on the back of the car. My mom didn't question the two bags and sleeping bag because I always brought a lot of video games and my console when I slept at Andy's.

This time, though, I was going numb-thumb deep without him.

I had packed my dad's heavy-duty flashlight plus

another, smaller one; extra batteries; and my pocket knife. Earlier in the day, I had walked to a nearby convenience store to buy snacks and energy drinks. The energy drinks were really expensive and I had spent like three weeks' worth of allowance on them, but we would need them for the long night ahead.

I shoved open the car door and jumped out without saying good-bye, but the image of Ms. Birch sobbing over her memories of Pirate Island made me hesitate. What if something happened to me? I didn't want my mom's last memory of me to be of me running out of the car without a good-bye.

I dropped my bags in the grass next to my bike and climbed across the passenger seat to give my mom a hug. "Bye, Mom. I love you." That was all good-boy Billy talking, but William (and Kidd) didn't seem to mind.

"I love you too, Billy." She ruffled my hair. "You go and have fun. And be good."

"I will," I said, though it was a lie.

Now that I had said a proper farewell, I was ready to start my adventure on Pirate Island. It was a little after 6:00 p.m. and time to get to the beach.

The air was heavy like on the day Kristina and I went to Ms. Birch's. I hoped we wouldn't get any storms. I slipped on my backpack, slung my duffel bag over one shoulder, and set the straps of my sleeping bag case over the other, and then precariously set off on my bike. Five minutes in, sweat soaked my shirt and dripped down my face. Thankfully it wasn't long before I arrived at the beach.

There it was: Pirate Island, a dark smudge of land against the bright blue sky. The sun hung low to my right, but its rays didn't seem to reach the island.

While I waited for Kristina and Justin, I thought about Kidd's spirit possessing me and how Andy had gotten me into this whole mess. That was when Andy showed up and Kristina spilled her little secret about inviting him.

Despite all that, I am now on the tombolo heading to Pirate Island, a reproduction of the original map secured in a waterproof folder in one of my bags. My destiny—our destiny—a few sandy steps away on a 14-acre stretch of land.

A tiny thought forms in my head, but I tuck it away as my neck begins to prickle. Kidd is here, listening, waiting. And there are some things I can't let him know.

Chapter 38

Letting the wind drown out any conversation between the others behind me, I breathe in the salty air of Long Island Sound. It calms my nerves as much as it creates a little bubble of excitement in my stomach. No, not just mine. Ours—mine and Kidd's—always *ours* now.

There are a few boats out on the water this evening, enjoying the last of the daylight. If they were so inclined, they could see us walking across the small strip of sand to Pirate Island. As I worry someone might notice us, a heavy fog moves across the water, blocking us from the boaters' view. It's as if I've summoned it, but I don't have that kind of power. Does Kidd?

I look back along the tombolo and find only fog. The shapes of Kristina, Justin, and Andy materialize one by one. They look like ghosts, a part of the mist as much as emerging from it. Turning towards Pirate Island again, I find it's vanished in the fog as well. I focus on taking in the sand, rocks, and shells in front of me, moving one step at a time closer to the island.

The air is thick and menacing. Buckets of sweat drip down my back. The straps of my bags and sleeping bag dig into my shoulders. I carry on until the beach widens in front of me. As I take that first step onto Pirate Island, a little tingle travels up my legs, into my fingertips, and all the way to the top of my head.

We are here at last, the closest we have been to finding treasure. Two steps farther and I break through the haze. The whole island is revealed from my vantage point, but it is surrounded by mist, masking it from outsiders.

Once again, I am breaking the law by being on the island during nesting season. I am sure I'm about to break a whole bunch of others by digging here. I inhale the salty brine of low tide and let it soak into my brain, feeling like a real pirate.

"Where to now?" Kristina asks as she appears out of the haze. Justin quickly follows, and finally Andy comes into sight.

I glare at Andy and talk to the other two. "We should set up camp on the interior of the island. Then we need to pinpoint where to dig because the sun will set soon and it looks like it's going to be extra dark tonight."

In my backpack, I find a pair of wire cutters I stole from my dad. I step up to the flimsy orange fence and cut through it without a second thought to the fact that I'm destroying public property.

Andy grins with that stupid smirk he does, seemingly

recovered from my slight. He marches into the trees like he owns the place. Kristina and Lover Boy, their free hands clasped together all mushy like, follow Andy.

"Captain Kidd," I whisper to myself, "please let us find your treasure tonight." I head towards the trees, but stop before I reach them. In my head, I tell him, "And I hope your spirit finds its way to the next world, or whatever it is your looking for."

"William!" Kristina yells from behind the trees. "You coming?"

I plunge through the overgrown branches and hike my way to the clearing in the center of the island. Kristina sits on one of her bags, supervising as Justin and Andy pitch the tent. The setting sun is behind the haze, so it's already dark enough in the clearing that they're using flashlights in order to see what they're doing. I set down my bags next to Kristina and let them figure out the logistics of camp.

I'm the captain here and have more important things to worry about. Using my dad's flashlight, I study the copy of the map, examining the rocks and the 62 P and 66 P. I orientate myself with a compass, which I bought at the hardware store as my dad doesn't have one, and flash the light in the direction we need to go.

Once the tent is ready, I turn to Kristina. "You ready?" She swallows and nods, uncharacteristically silent. "Take your flashlight and follow me."

"What about us?" asks Andy.

"Finish setting up and then do whatever you want." I throw the comment over my shoulder, not bothering to turn around.

"That's harsh," Kristina says as we head towards the 62 P rock.

Not that I need to defend my actions, but I offer her an explanation. "He's been like that to me forever. Bossing me around, getting me into all these crazy adventures that never turn into anything, and never caring about what I want. I'm sick of it. He deserves some of his own treatment."

"Maybe," she says. "But don't you always have fun on those crazy adventures? It's not really about what it leads to in the end, right?"

It's a good point to consider, but I'm not in the mood to give an inch when it comes to Andy. Arriving at the east edge of the island and cutting through the fence again saves me from having to answer. I scan the many rocks. With the map, it's almost too easy to find the right one now that I know what to look for. I shine the light on a huge boulder flanked by two smaller ones and point it south to find three smaller rocks in a triangular formation.

Putting the largest boulder back in the light, I tell her, "It's this one you want to start from. Remember to take big, man-sized steps for your sixty-two paces."

It can't be easy for Kristina to take orders from me,

her little brother, but all she says is, "I remember."

"You've got your walkie-talkie?" She nods, and I pat my pocket and feel mine beneath the fabric. I cut a space through the fence for her. "I'll radio you when I get to the other rock."

With the island still shrouded in mist, I slowly make my way around the beach because the sky is an inky black now. There is a full moon tonight, but it's not making an appearance past the mounting clouds.

Despite the dark, it's easy to find the 66 P rock, which has a circle of five smaller rocks surrounding it. Canvassing the island before was overwhelming when I didn't have the map to guide me. I silently thank Ms. Birch for giving me the right tool (and Kidd for giving me the courage to steal it).

I determine the direction I need to head before making a space in the fence for myself. Standing at my rock, I radio Kristina. "I'm in position. You copy?"

"Roger," comes her staticky response.

I like how seriously she's taking this. "We go after three. Copy?"

"Copy, Roger that." She might be taking it a little too far now, but whatever, I have a treasure to find.

I count down on the walkie-talkie, clip it on my waistband, and begin taking my paces. Exaggerating my steps as much as I can, I count them out loud to keep track.

There are a few tricky spots of thick brambles I have

to navigate through and I almost lose my count. I make it past a bunch of trees, doing my best to keep a straight line, and continue to the edge of the clearing. The tent is on the far end, a lantern lighting up our camp. Justin and Andy pause their card game and watch my progress.

Kristina comes through the trees to the right of camp. I stop. I hold five fingers out on one hand and four on the other to remind myself that I'm on pace number 54.

"What number are you at?" I ask.

"Fifty-one, fifty-two, fifty-three," she says out loud.

I continue my paces and stop at 66, almost in the center of the clearing. Kristina halts about fifteen feet from me and a little to the north. It would take days to dig a hole that big if we go the planned six-feet deep, a morbid depth, but based on what Ms. Birch said, I know it has to be at least as deep as an average man.

"What now?" she asks as Justin and Andy come over to take a look.

Justin stands in between Kristina and I. He stretches his arms out and doesn't come close to reaching either of us. "That's a big hole," he says.

Now Justin is acting like a captain, Captain Obvious.

My pirate rage rises, but I swallow it down and take a deep breath. "We're not going to dig a hole that big."

"So where are we going to dig then?" asks Kristina.

Good question. Too bad I have no idea how to answer.

Chapter 39

Closing my eyes, I try to channel Kidd's spirit. I flip off my shoes, heedless of the rats I know reside on Pirate Island, and sink my feet into the loamy dirt. *Talk to me, Kidd.*

A buzzing sensation fills my limbs and gathers in my chest. Eyes still closed, I suck in a breath and take two steps forward before stumbling to the left. I fall on my hands and knees and finally open my eyes. I'm light-headed and sweaty from the effort. A draining fatigue makes my limbs shake ever so slightly.

Kristina is staring at me, her mouth hanging open in surprise. Justin looks kind of impressed, though it's hard to tell with him because I've never seen much emotion cross his face, not unless you count pained musician, which I don't.

I avoid looking at Andy, but he refuses to be ignored. "Dude, that was freaky."

On my knees, I mark a big X in the dirt with the handle of the flashlight. "This is where we dig."

A breeze swoops through the trees, erasing my X. A splotch of rain lands on my hand, quickly followed by another on my nose. I grab three sticks and force them deep into the earth as a more permanent marker than a scraping in the sand.

"Uh," Kristina says. "Did anyone check the weather?"

"Sixty percent chance of thunderstorms," says Andy. We all turn towards him. He shrugs. "I thought it might be important."

Who is this person who comes prepared with a weather report? Certainly not my ex-best friend who normally flies by the seat of his pants...when they're not being torn up on barbed wire fences.

Thunder rumbles in the distance.

Kristina heads to the tent. "I'll be in there if you need me."

Justin dutifully follows her, and they disappear inside. I'm about to as well, but Andy beats me to it, slipping past the zipper and leaving it open for me. My sister, her boyfriend, and my ex-best friend: that's a trio I don't care to join. I consider staying outside with my duo (one body, two souls) and waiting out the weather.

Then lightning flashes across the sky and the drizzle turns into a steady rain. I decide to take my chances in the tent. I blow out the lantern and tuck it under a bush, hoping it doesn't get blown over and break.

It's a tight fit in the tent, and I squeeze into a corner

to avoid touching knees with anyone. Lover Boy has his guitar out—I guess he takes it everywhere with him—and begins playing a sappy-sounding song.

"Oh." Kristina claps and stares dreamily at him. "It's my song. He wrote this for me."

I roll my eyes at Andy and quickly look away when I remember we're not friends. The truce we came to the other night over Kung Pao isn't enough to erase years of bossing me around (or Kidd's suspicion of him).

Justin's singing voice isn't bad, but the lyrics— something about deep love and whispers—are so sappy... and gross because they're about my sister. It's torture, pure torture. I'd rather face the noose than listen to this. Where's a bucket when you need one?

The storm kicks up a notch as Justin sings on. Wind rattles the canvas. Lightning flashes, and it's bright enough to be noon on a sunny day. Thunder crashes so loudly that it drowns out all other sounds and leaves my ears ringing. I cover my ears, my only solace that I can no longer hear Lover Boy's song.

I silently prayed to Kidd, one William to another. *Please, please, please let the storm stop before midnight.*

My neck tingles, and I take that as a good sign. Then my ears recover and Lover Boy is in full force, him moaning away and Kristina melting. We're in for a long night.

Chapter 40

The storm rocks the tent and all of us in it. There is so much rain that it starts to leak through the canvas, soaking us any time we touch it. We huddle closer to the middle. A steady drip of water makes it through the ceiling, and we end up soaked within minutes.

The one ray of sunshine is that the storm has forced Lover Boy to put his guitar away. I'm happy for about one minute until the next thunderclap booms. I jump from the sound and hit the side of the tent, shaking it so it pours water down on us. Kristina squeals, and then there's silence. I think everyone is as scared as I am.

Where is Kidd's bravery when I need it?

Finally, after an hour of torrential downpours, blinding lightning, and earth-rumbling thunder, the storm blows itself out. We stay in the tent until the steady drips die down. At least the ground will be nice and soft for digging.

I consider reaching out to Kidd again to gauge how we're doing, but Andy interrupts my attempt. "I'm bored."

Justin pats his guitar case. "I could play some more."

"No!" I yell. Kristina punches me in the arm with a pointed look. "It's just, ummm...I want to be able to hear what's going on outside. Why don't we play a game?"

"A game?" She laughs. "What kind of game?"

I try to think of a game that would be cool, but all I can think of is I Spy, and that is definitely not cool.

"How about Truth or Dare," Andy suggests.

Truth or Dare with my sister and her boyfriend? I don't think so.

I'm sure Kristina will agree with me until she says, "Okay. I'll pick first. Justin, truth or dare?"

"Dare," he says.

"I dare you to run around outside with nothing but your boxers on," she says.

In my head, I plead with Kidd to get in here and do something about this. But there's no response. Is he gone for good? Maybe that's not a bad thing for me to no longer be possessed. But it's definitely bad no one's here to stop Justin from running around in his boxers.

Thankfully, Andy steps up. "Forget it!" he shouts. "Pick again."

Surprisingly, Justin nods in agreement.

"All right. I have something even better." Kristina reaches into her bag and pulls a little bottle out of it. "I dare you to let me paint your nails. That way we'll match."

She holds up her fingers and wiggles them, showing

off her traffic-cone orange nails.

"Okay," he agrees. "I'm not sure how that'll work over black." He holds up his own jet-black nails.

Lover Boy is too much; I can't believe Kristina is so in love with him. I bust out laughing at the same exact time as Andy, which cuts me right off. He falls silent, and I feel his gaze burning a hole in me. I won't look. I can't handle the smoke-and-mirrors act. I'm sure I'll fall for it like I always used to.

Aside from the continual patter of rain, it's quiet in the tent. And stinky as Kristina paints Justin's nails.

"You're turn to ask," she says to him while she works.

"William," he says, and my stomach does a somersault, "truth or dare?"

With the threat of orange fingernails hanging over me, I choose truth. He opens his mouth, hesitates, and then clamps it shut. He looks to Kristina, but she's focused on his hands.

When he opens his mouth again, there's a rush of words. "Do you really think there's pirate treasure on this island?"

He says it like he doesn't believe it. Like I'm crazy to believe. Like he can't believe anyone could be so stupid to think there is pirate treasure on the island. I totally agree that I'm crazy, but not because I think we're going to find buried treasure on Pirate Island tonight. Nope, I'm crazy because I have a pirate spirit possessing me. Or at least I did.

So what does the crazy, possessed Captain William do? He tells the truth; that's the name of the game after all.

Chapter 41

I answer Justin's question about whether or not I believe we'll find treasure on Pirate Island with a voice-cracking "yes" that makes me sound unsure, though I'm firm in my beliefs.

"Really?" he asks

Afraid my voice will crack again, I nod with authority.

Feeling more confident, I say, "At first I wasn't sure." I recall the first time I opened my favorite biography and inhaled the cloud of dust. "Even when I read all those books about Captain Kidd and I saw that letter that he had all this treasure hidden away somewhere, I wasn't sure."

I wasn't sure then, but Kidd had already been pushing me to find the treasure right from the start. "Then Kristina and I talked to Ms. Birch. She definitely experienced something crazy on this island. Then there was the letter that said Captain Kidd had been in our town, that he had sailed his ship right by here. It's just too many coincidences not to mean something. And the map. We wouldn't be here without the map." (And without Kidd's spirit.)

Everyone stares at me for a moment. The dripping rain counts off the silent seconds. Justin shrugs. "Your turn."

Ignoring Andy, I challenge Kristina, and she picks dare. I offer her an energy drink and dare her to chug it.

"That is so gross," she says. "And so immature. I'm not doing it, and I pick you. William, truth or dare?"

Stupidly, I continue to hold the energy drink out to her. "No fair. You can't skip your turn and ask me again."

"I don't care," she says. "It's your fault I'm out here on this awful island in the rain, so I say it's my turn, and I pick you. Truth or dare?"

I narrow my eyes, willing Captain William to defy her. Instead I concede. "Fine. Dare."

Kristina taps her lip before deciding. "How about you chug that energy drink?"

I crack open the can and chug. I swallow as fast as I can, but bubbles rise up the back of my throat and into my nose. Fluid shoots out of my mouth and nose and sprays all over her.

She screams. Andy is cracking up, and even Justin looks like he's holding back laughter.

"You are so gross!" she yells. "I'm out of here."

"Wait!" The word shoots out of my mouth without me thinking. I look at my watch. It's 11:45, only 15 minutes until we start digging. "It's time to get ready."

Chapter 42

We file out of the tent to find the rain has almost completely stopped. Kristina refuses to help bring the supplies to the digging site, so Justin, Andy, and I gather the shovels and drinks near the marking sticks. The lantern made it through the storm intact, so I relight it and set it nearby. Using the shovel handle, I make a big circle to indicate how big a hole we should dig. The activity (or maybe Kidd) keeps my nerves at bay.

We've gone over this already, but I say, "Remember, once midnight hits, absolutely no talking."

Justin picks up a shovel, and I offer the last one to Kristina.

She shakes her head. "Nope. I'm not digging."

"What?" Blood boiling (yup, Kidd is definitely back), I consider whacking her on the head with the shovel, which would do a lot more damage than a bucket. "You have to. We need three diggers. You promised."

She grabs the shovel from me, giving me hope, only to dash it a moment later when she shoves it at Andy. "He can dig. Why else do you think I asked him to come?"

"I thought...because we were fighting..." I stammer. She turns her back on us and retreats to the tent. "Whatever." As long as we have three people digging, I don't care if one of them is Andy. So long as he keeps his hands off the loot when we find it.

I check my watch. 11:55. Five minutes to go. My heart beats like I've just outrun an opponent to the soccer ball. I show Justin and Andy the signal I'll use to let them know to start.

11:56. Four minutes until we break ground.

I wonder what we'll find in the earth. Will it be what Kidd is looking for? Will it be what I'm looking for (whatever that is, I'm not sure anymore)? Will I ever be rid of this dual personality or will I spend the rest of my life as Captain William?

Perhaps my life will come to an end tonight, here on Pirate Island. There are enough stories about tragedy to make it a real possibility. Ms. Birch's old beau George, the Native Americans who sold the whole town for some worthless items, the hotel that burned here. And Captain William Kidd, of course. He didn't die on the island, but his is the most tragic story I know.

11:57.

Chapter 43

Two minutes to go.

It's very quiet. I can't even hear the waves from this part of the island. I kind of miss the thunder. Then I take the thought back. We don't need any complications.

11:59.

I grip my shovel so tightly that my knuckles turn white. The thud, thud, thud of my pounding heart explodes in my ears. I take a few quiet breaths, not that it helps me feel any calmer. If anything it makes me light-headed. I force myself to focus on the bright numbers on my watch.

I'm Captain William. I'm a pirate. I'm a pirate. I'm a pirate.

12:00.

I push the tip of my shovel into the soil and force it down with my boot, the signal for the others to start. Andy and Justin strike dirt a moment later. Then we get down to work. Plunge the shovel into the dirt, push it farther down, and toss the soil out of the hole. The work creates a beat in my head: plunge push toss, plunge push toss, plunge push toss. It blocks out any emotions running inside of me (or Kidd).

The air is thick with moisture. Sweat drips down my face into the dirt. The bugs have the pleasure of making the flesh of my neck their dinner. I work my hardest—and I hate to admit this—but Justin's part of the hole is the deepest. Andy's part is only a little bit deeper than mine. Not that it matters. It's not a contest, though I still want to win. I push myself harder.

We go on like that for hours. Digging, digging, digging. We barely stop to drink. After the energy drinks are long gone and we're running low on water, we keep on digging. Kristina has joined us, as has the moon. They both stare silently down upon us and our growing hole.

I'm beyond tired. My jelly arms shake each time I strike the ground. The bottom of my foot throbs every time I push the shovel down with my boot. Each shovelful of dirt that needs to be hauled up and out of the hole feels heavier than the last.

My neck is slick with sweat, but no tingles or prickles of the noose Kidd wore. He is silent. I worry that he has abandoned me and also hopeful that he has.

What if we keep digging forever and never find anything? How do I decide when it's time to stop?

A glance at my watch tells me it's 3:48 a.m. At 4:00, I think, we'll stop. Treasure or no treasure.

My body moves on auto-pilot, though a very painful

one. The minutes creep closer and closer to the stopping time. I push my shovel into the dirt for what must be the four billionth time. A loud thunk echoes in the deep hole. My hands vibrate and my heart flutters with the pressure of finally hitting something solid.

Chapter 44

Kristina sucks in a loud breath. Justin, Andy, and I all look up and glare at her. Peering into the hole, she mouths "sorry."

I get on my knees and work by hand to free the object. There isn't room for Justin and Andy to bend down, so they stand by and watch. I'm not able to ask for more light, but Kristina has the sense to shine one of the flashlights down into the hole.

I try not the think of Ms. Birch holding a flashlight over a different hole on a night long ago as I scoop and scrape at the dirt.

Finally, I uncover the top of a wooden chest. I'm hotter and sweatier than I have ever been in my whole life, but goose bumps prickle my arms. My body heaves with exhaustion as I work to free the sides of the chest, but there is strength in me yet. Perhaps Kidd is sending me extra energy. His presence is a boon while also a burden.

When I unearth a handle on the side of the chest, I grabbed it and pull with all my might. It comes up so easily, either Kidd has sent me super strength or the chest is way lighter than expected. The momentum flings me backward into Justin and Andy. We fall in a heap of body parts, topped by the treasure chest.

The weight is lifted off of us. I peer up to see Kristina hauling the chest over the edge of the hole. So it must be light, not that I have super strength. Curious, very curious. A knot of nervousness twists my stomach. Could it be empty?

Justin gives Andy a boost out, and then Kristina offers a hand to help Justin. I'm waiting for her to do the same for me when Andy reaches down towards me. I hesitate, or Kidd does. But I ultimately take his hand and let him help me up. He is—*was*—my best friend.

The chest beckons me, and it's all I see in the moonlight. It doesn't look how I imagined it would, and I've spent a lot of time envisioning this moment. I expected it to be engraved with gold and jewels with a big skull and crossbones on top. Instead, it's a plain brown, very dirty, and slightly soggy wooden box. I run my hand over the top and feel little grooves all along the wood.

Andy, Kris, and Justin all stare at me in awe. It's an unspoken agreement that we remain silent.

I put my hand out and Kristina gives me the flashlight. The light reveals the grooves to be pictures. One is a bird with a skinny body and long, stick-like legs; another is a simple canoe; and a third is a feather. There are also letters engraved on the sides of the chest, but if they form words, they aren't in any language I know. I wait to see if maybe Kidd will translate them, but he's as mum as we are.

A big lock seals the lid. Andy shoves me and jumps up and down, and I find his enthusiasm contagious despite myself (and Kidd). A light sheen of sweat covers Kristina's forehead. I don't think I've seen her sweat before. She gestures with her hand as if to say, "Go on and open it."

Of course I'm the one who should open the treasure chest. So why don't I get to it already?

My hands shake as I reach for the lock. It's so old and rusty that a single poke with my pocketknife busts it open. Body heat presses down on me as Andy, Kristina, and Justin lean in close. No one speaks. I am so afraid that any noise will turn the whole adventure to disaster that I barely breathe. I clutch the sides of the lid and pry it open.

Chapter 45

The lid squeaks as it opens, breaking the careful quiet we've been maintaining for hours. It's worse than train wheels screeching on metal tracks. It's worse than that horrible noise the egret made the day Kristina and I freed it from the lobster pot. It's worse than Justin's band!

The noise is forgotten as the lid reaches the pinnacle and swings all the way open. White light surrounds us. The light—or another, unseen force—pushes me on my back and pins me to the ground. Shadowy figures emerge from the glow.

I'm trapped and helpless on the ground of Pirate Island with strange figures looming over me, and all I can think is, "I thought the light was supposed to be blue, not white."

A hand brushes my arm, and I squeal in fright. Scaredy-boy Billy is back, and there's no sign of Captain William.

Bright orange fingernails dig into my skin, and I can breathe again as I recognize them as Kristina's. I grab her hand. It's kind of corny, but I'm less scared while holding hands with my sister. The light dims and the pressure decreases enough for us to stand. Andy and Justin are also getting to their feet.

Unfortunately, the figures don't disappear with the fading light. They are bare-chested and have long hair. The figures circle around, forcing us closer together. They begin to chant.

Holding Kristina's hand, I find my other hand reaching out for Andy's. Justin grasps both Kristina's and Andy's hands, and we form a tight circle. It's like we've all become possessed (not just me) and are acting in ways our bodies can't control. There's no other way to describe what we're doing.

The shadowy figures dance in a circle, kind of hopping and flailing their arms in time with their chanting. It's hypnotic and terrifying.

The four of us firmly hold hands. Together we rotate in the opposite direction of the dancing. We're a spinning top, going faster than I thought possible. Everything, except for my fellow treasure hunters' faces, turns to a blur.

We stop, or maybe we're spinning so fast that I can't tell we're moving. Then it's all gone: the faces, the Natives (that's the only explanation of who those figures must be), the chanting, the whole island has disappeared.

I am lost, floating in a gray fog. In dead silence. Maybe I am dead. Maybe Kidd's spirit finally crossed over and took me with it.

Time passes. I don't know how much. The world is fog and nothing more.

Chapter 46

A shout comes from the distance, reaching out through the blank gray infinity. It's a shout of joy. A fuzzy shape forms in the haze. A man in a football helmet appears, the number 13 printed on his jersey. He leaps up and down—seemingly more anchored to the ground than I am—and hollers, "We won! We won! Champ·i·ons! Champ·i·ons!"

The roar of an invisible crowd surrounds us. The man seems to be able to see them, but I don't think he can see me. He pulls off his helmet and holds it up in a triumphant pose, like he's the fake gold guy on top of a trophy. His sweaty blond hair hangs almost to his shoulders. A faint scar runs from his right eyebrow halfway to the hairline above his ear.

I blink in shock. It's Andy, only Andy like I have never seen him before. An ugly scar on his face. And all grown up. His image blurs. When he solidifies again, he's wearing different clothes and his clean hair is pulled back in a low ponytail. He sits on a stool, speaking...no, reciting a poem. He finishes and more invisible people clap. He says, "Thank you. Now here's one I wrote sophomore year."

Wait. Did Andy—the quarterback, my tough (ex?) best friend, the guy who was too cool for pirates—just say he wrote a poem? And was he reading it in front of an audience? Before I can speak to him (not that he would hear me) he fades back into the fog.

"Wait!" I yell, but it's lost in the gray world.

A woman appears. She has black hair with neon-orange streaks and a pierced nose. Rock music blasts around us, but of course, I can't see anything but the woman. She sings into a microphone, "He don't love me anymore!" She sings the line over and over until it turns into a scream.

It's more haunting than any ghost story. It's beautiful, and heartbreaking.

She looks up, right into my eyes, and stops screaming. A single tear falls from her eye, smearing black makeup down her cheek. I stare into those eyes and know them. They are my sister's. I reach out a hand to Kristina, to wipe the tear from her face, but she smiles and disappears into the fog.

My hand grabs nothing but air. I am alone again. I should be scared, I would be, but I'm not able to feel anything. My mind is numb. My body is cold. I don't understand what is happening. Where am I? Why am I seeing these images? What are they?

Chapter 47

I can't voice these questions, and it doesn't matter because the fog has something new in store for me.

My dad steps out of it. Only his hair and face are a little off, maybe he's an older version of himself like the others. No, he looks younger than my dad. He walks closer to me. A woman follows behind. My dad whispers in her ear and kisses her smack on the lips.

My heart skips a beat. At least I still have a heart!

The woman's face is blocked by my dad's, but it definitely isn't my mom's. Her hair is the wrong color and she's too tall. My stomach churns. I don't want to be seeing this, or any of these visions...whatever they are. I don't want this one to be true.

The woman laughs, and it echoes through the mist. "Oh, Bill," she says. "I love you, too."

My brain is about to squeeze right out of my ears; that's how much this is making my head hurt. The woman said Bill, not my dad's name. Bill, short for William.

That can only mean that was me—future me. Was

that my girlfriend, or even weirder, my wife? It's not possible. None of this is possible.

Am I seeing the future as it will be or as it could be? Am I hallucinating and this is all a bunch of nonsense? Maybe I hit my head. Kidd...he must have something to do with this.

And where are Andy, Kristina, and Justin?

I am crying, the hot tears on my face are the only things I can feel through the numbness. There is no pirate left in me. Kidd would slice his sword through the mist, kill anyone in his way, and rescue his friends. He managed to kill a man with a bucket, surely he could handle a little fog and a few ghostly figures.

But I'm not Kidd. I may have borrowed his persona for a while, but I've never truly been Captain William.

I resort to beating my hands on my chest like a chimpanzee and yelling like a madman, "Ahhhh, uhhhh, uhhhh! Who's out there? Why are you showing me these things? I hate you. Go away! Go away!"

The words are sucked up by the fog. There isn't even an echo. Just silence. Deep, cold silence. All I want is to be home in my bed with a good book waiting for me under my pillow, one that has nothing to do with pirates or lost treasure or ghosts.

That's when I realize something very important. It's a lightning-bolt moment, minus the frizzy hair and shock.

Captain Kidd—mighty pirate and accused murderer—

didn't manage to escape his own fate of the noose. When the rope broke the first time, they strung him back up, though it was supposed to be a sign to let him be free. Kidd wasn't superhuman. He was a man, one that did terrible things in his life, true pirate or not. Not the kind of guy that should be revered.

I no longer care about what Captain Kidd would do or if he is possessing me. I'm not Kidd or Captain William. I'm William Bonny. A 13-year-old kid who has done some pretty amazing things in the past few weeks. I lost my best friend and (maybe) gained him back. I punched a varsity football player and lived to talk about it. I did a ton of research and a found an ancient treasure—it might not be pirate treasure, but whatever we have uncovered on Pirate Island is special, that's for sure.

It's never been a matter of me needing Kidd for courage or strength. It's always been a matter of me finding it within myself. With that bolt of brain lightning, I decide to find my way back home, or at least back to Pirate Island.

Chapter 48

The images may be nothing more than mist, but I'm not. I'm made of solid flesh and bone. As soon as I realize this, the sensation in my legs comes back. There is ground beneath my boots again.

The fog surrounds me, but I'm not afraid. I make swimming motions with my arms and slowly walk forward. I focus on trying to move in one direction, squinting my eyes as they detect a bright light breaking through the mist.

It's not the light you see right before you die, I'm sure of that, so I head towards it.

That's when I hear a sound that I know is real, not voices from the future. It's the quiet lapping of water on the shore. My feet reach the water, and it soaks through my boots. The light is coming from a point out in the water. A warm breeze tickles my arms and blows the fog away. In front of me is Long Island Sound, and beyond that the shoreline of the mainland spreads out in a crescent shape. The sun peeks out over the water horizon.

I back up until my boots touch sand and plunk down on my butt. Pulling off my boots and socks, I release my feet and squish my toes in the sand. The sun warms my face as it rises. It's never felt better to experience such small comforts.

The memories of the visions wash over me. Andy the champion, Andy the poet. Kristina the heart-broken rocker chick. Me all grown-up, a girl—no, a woman—telling me she loves me. Have I seen the future? I don't know. Maybe it's a possible version of the future. Maybe it was all a dream. It doesn't matter.

The visions made me realize it's okay to be me. I don't have to be jealous of Andy for being a super-jock. I have my own set of talents; some I probably don't know about yet. I will never stop worrying about Kristina—and will probably hate all the guys she dates—but she is strong and can take care of herself.

The visions have freed me from Kidd (if he really was possessing me at all). I can face the scary, the unknown, and be brave all on my own. I have a wide-open future in front of me, whether that is the one I saw in the vision or a different one altogether.

Either way, I'm not going to face that future being afraid. I'm going to be my true self. I'm not quite sure what that means, but I'm going to try and figure that out.

I'm deep in thought when sand rustles behind me. It's Kristina, looking like her normal, present-day self. She sits down next to me, crosses her legs, and leans back on her hands.

Closing her eyes, she says, "Did you go somewhere last night after we opened the treasure chest?" I nod, though she can't see me with her eyes closed, but I think she senses it. Her next words come slowly, like she doesn't quite believe them. "Did you see things? Images. Of the future?"

I nod again. We sit in silence and watch the sun creep farther into the sky.

"I saw you," I finally say.

"You did?" Kristina asks, the surprise clear in her voice.

"Yeah. And you weren't with," I make my voice sound all girly and high-pitched, "dreamy Justin."

I pay for the joke with a punch in the arm. Yup, my sister can definitely take care of herself. I rub my arm as she quietly laughs.

"Well, whatever that was it sure was crazy." She pauses and squints at the water. "Do you think it was real?"

I shrug, feeling serious again. "Does it matter if it was?"

"I guess not. I know what it made me feel, and that was real even if the images weren't."

"Yeah." I don't think I need to say anything more.

Chapter 49

A beautiful day is dawning, the sky a lighter version of the deep blue waters of Long Island Sound. A majestic white bird flies overhead. Kristina and I exchange a smile because we know egrets don't look so majestic on the ground. I dig my feet deeper into the sand.

I'm not ready to break the bubble of contentment, but a familiar voice calls out, "Dude! That was awesome!"

Andy and Justin emerge from the trees and join us. I'm happy to have my best friend on one side of me and my sister on the other. Andy is talking away, and I'm half-listening, just like old times.

Kristina and Justin are deep in conversation. He keeps saying, "Man, that was so trippy."

I'm so content, I don't even feel like puking when Justin kisses Kristina. I simply look away out at the water.

A glint of sunlight reflects off my watch. The time reads 6:53 a.m.

"Guys," I say. "Low tide is in fourteen minutes. We better pack up and get across the sandbar before we miss the window."

"Andy and I packed up camp," Justin said. "When I got out of that trance-thingy, I figured I'd start cleaning up. Andy stumbled into the clearing and helped. Then we came to find you." He holds tight to Kristina's hand.

Who would've figured Justin ends up being the responsible one?

In the clearing, I stop and stare at the place where we dug the hole. There's no sign of it or the treasure chest.

Andy punches me on the shoulder. "It's all gone. Disappeared without a trace. Freaky, right?"

I shake my head. I'm beginning to believe in all those ghost stories about Pirate Island.

We shoulder the supplies and make our way to the sandbar, which is still plenty wide enough for us to cross without worrying about drowning. Along the way, Andy tells me all about the plan he came up with to sneak out of his house to come here.

He set up a tent in the tiny backyard behind the condo and told his dad he was camping out for the night. So Justin is going to drop us off a block away from Andy's condo, and we're going to sneak back into the tent. Hopefully our parents won't have a clue where we really were.

When we get to the car, I toss my stuff in the trunk along with my bike. Then I settle into the back seat next to my best friend. We zip away from the beach, Justin's stupid music blaring from the speakers. It doesn't bother me so much anymore.

Twisting in my seat, I watch Pirate Island out the rear windshield. The reflection of the sun makes it look like the water all around the island is on fire. Pirate Island is a bluish green oasis in the flames.

I wonder if Captain Kidd's ghost haunts it now or if it ever did. The Native ghosts certainly do. Is there enough room on that small island for so many spirits? I'm okay with never finding out the answer to that question. I sigh and lean back into the seat.

I hold out my fist to Andy. "Numb-thumb deep."

He pounds my fist. "No kidding. Numbest thumb I've ever had."

Chapter 50

A few days later—two days before the start of eighth grade—I arrive at the library extra early for the last writing class of the summer. I hustle to the research section, searching not for a book but for a person.

I find him sorting a stack of old books in a quiet corner, the name Ken stitched on his collared shirt. His sleek dark hair and sharp nose remind me of the shadowy figures on Pirate Island. I almost expected not to find him, like he was a ghost, too. But there he is, flesh and bone.

"It really shouldn't be called Pirate Island, should it." It's not a question.

Ken stares down at me with his deep brown eyes, his lips unsuccessfully trying to hide a smile. "Well, I'm not sure I know what you mean, William."

"No, you do." I give him a hint of a smile back. "But it's illegal to dig on the misnamed island, so we can pretend we don't know anything about that, right?"

"What did you expect to find?" he asks. "Pirate treasure? More like six coats, ten blankets, one kettle, twelve hatchets, twelve hoes, two dozen knives, and," I chime in with him, "a dozen mirrors."

His face brightens in a full-on smirk, but then it squints up in a serious way. "Seems you were lucky this time, but I wouldn't be going out there again if I were you. You never know what you'll find next time. Not all the ghosts on that island are so forgiving."

I think of Ms. Birch, her brother, and her beau George. Two dead, one living in fear of Pirate Island. "I don't think I'll be going out there again. I've had my fill of ghosts for a while."

He shakes his head in approval. "Good. Very good."

I check my watched and apologize for having to go. Class starts in one minute, but before I go, I say one more thing to Ken. "You can call me Bill."

He waves. "Sure thing, Bill."

Ignoring library rules, I run to class and join Andy in the back. The party has already started, and everyone is hanging around talking and enjoying the snacks.

Mrs. Shields stands at the front of the room and claps to get our attention.

A smile bigger than Andy's signature grin is plastered on her face. "I have a very special announcement. One of our very own will be having his poem published in a professional literary journal." Heads swivel around to see who has earned such a distinguished honor. I know who it is before Mrs. Shields says the name. "C'mon, Andy. Stand up and let us all congratulate you."

The class breaks into a raucous applause. Ella, the most beautiful girl in class—the most beautiful girl I know —claps the loudest of all. A tiny voice whispers in my head. *He's a fake, a phony. He cheated. No way he wrote something good enough to be published. School's your thing, not Andy's.*

I swat my hand next to my ear, brushing away the jealousy. I, Bill Bonny, am happy for my best friend, even if it means he truly does beat me at everything...even school! I push my chair away from the table and stand, giving Andy the ovation he deserves. The rest of the class copies me.

Ella flashes me a smile and blows a big, pink bubble with her gum. Maybe one day I'll have the courage to talk to her.

The class settles down and gets back to munching on snacks and chatting. As Andy and I work our way through an entire plate of brownies, he says through a full mouth, "You know, we never did find it. It could still be out there."

"What?" I ask.

He smacks me on the head. "Duh. The pirate treasure. We could go look for it again."

"I think I've found enough treasure to last me a while."

"What do you mean?" He looks dumbfounded. "We didn't find anything."

I stare at the table full of girls and shrug. No time like

the present for talking to pretty girls. I show Andy my teeth and ask, "Do I have chocolate stuck anywhere?"

"Nah. You're good." He slaps me on the back. "Go for it, dude."

I go right up to Ella and tell her I liked the poem she read in class last week. She glances at her friends, who are all giggling, and then gestures to an empty table and asks if I want to sit. She splits her cookie in half and offers it to me. My stomach is busting from all the brownies, but I accept it and take a bite.

I glance back at Andy, and he gives me a thumbs up. I've certainly gone numb-thumb deep.

He was wrong about not finding anything on Pirate Island. We found a lot more than treasure there, and I'm pretty sure every single one of us who was there knows it.

ACKNOWLEDGMENTS

First and foremost, I write books I want to read. But I publish books in the hopes that others will enjoy the world and characters I create. So thank you to all of the readers who spent their precious time with my words. I hope you enjoyed going on this adventure with me, Billy, and Captain Kidd.

Research was an important aspect of creating *Pirate Island*. Information and inspiration came from *An Historical Account of Charles Island: Milford, Connecticut* by Michael C. Dooling, *The Pirate Hunter: The True Story of Captain Kidd* by Richard Zacks, *Captain Kidd (Pirates)* by Sue Hamilton, *Captain Kidd and the War against the Pirates* by Robert Ritchie, and *History of the Colony of New Haven* by Edward R. Lambert. Like Andy's father, my own dad has a collection of newspaper clippings about Charles Island—the real island behind Pirate Island—that I confiscated and were an important tool in my research.

More thanks goes to my early readers and critiquers David, Kerrie, and old and new members of the Weston Writers Group. Also, thanks to fellow authors Kai Strand, Mary Waibel, and S. Usher Evans for advice, encouragement, and guidance on this strange process of self-publishing a novel. My mom, Debby, deserves a lot of credit for offering her very affordable proofreading services, and with her sharp eye spotted typos, missing words, and the importance of making sure Billy always knew where his bike was. Of course, any errors are my responsibility. Illustrator Susan Tait Porcaro (susantaitporcaro.com) left me speechless with the gorgeous artwork she created for the cover. And always a special thanks to my muse Kylene.

Finally, thank you to Batman, The Boy, The Prince, and The Gentleman, my personal group of live-in superheroes. You inspire me and humble me each and every day. You take care of me. Hugs and love and kisses.

ABOUT THE AUTHOR

Katie L. Carroll always says she began writing at a very sad time in her life after her sister Kylene unexpectedly passed away. The truth is Katie has been writing her whole life, and it was only after Kylene's death that she realized she wanted to pursue writing for kids and teens as a career. Since then writing has taken her to many wonderful places, real and imagined. She has had many jobs in her lifetime, including newspaper deliverer, hardware store cashier, physical therapy assistant, and puzzle magazine editor. She works from her home in Connecticut that is filled with the love and laughter of her sons and husband.

In addition to *Pirate Island*, Katie is the author of *Elixir Bound* and the forthcoming *Elixir Saved*. For more about Katie and her books, visit her website at katielcarroll.com.

CPSIA information can be obtained
at www.ICGtesting.com
Printed in the USA
FFHW021949200719
53736437-59436FF